GLIMPSES

GLIMPSES

by

ERIC PARTRIDGE

(Corrie Denison, pseud.)

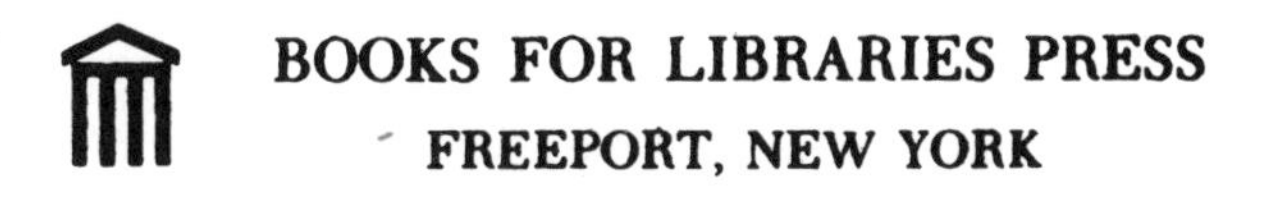

BOOKS FOR LIBRARIES PRESS
FREEPORT, NEW YORK

INTERNATIONAL STANDARD BOOK NUMBER:
0-8369-5707-5

LIBRARY OF CONGRESS CATALOG CARD NUMBER:
70-150194

PRINTED IN THE UNITED STATES OF AMERICA

TO

A. D. V.-P.

FOREWORD

When, as in these stories, many places are described or mentioned, it is only right that the author should state whether he has a first-hand knowledge or whether he relies mainly on hear-say or book-say. I would therefore like to state that I know them by having visited them, usually by having lived there for some time. With these two modifications : I do not claim the honour of having ever been a pupil at the Toowoomba Grammar School, but with the town I am familiar. And Dalby I have seen only twice, from the train as I was going to, and returning from, Roma on some government research-work : but my ignorance of the school and my wholly inadequate acquaintanceship with the town may perhaps be forgiven me when I add that I owe the matter of those two sections to an old friend of mine. As regards *A Mere Private* : this tale is neither drawn wholly from imagination nor based on a dead man's diary. The investigation of life in the lower quarters of Port Said, as casually recommended in *Charmian Warrington*, was considered very seriously by myself some years ago, but not only did circumstances prevent me from putting my plan into action but also I was not at all sure that, though I possessed all the requisites, I fulfilled all the requirements for such an undertaking. In respect of *A Tale of Three Cities*, it is necessary to say that, while I know Oxford very well as a visitor and have some good friends there, I owe the details of student life to a younger brother who went through a course several years after the war. In *Vernon Ditchley*, I have drawn on my mixed experiences as the representative of a publishing firm in London and the provinces in 1920, as a journalist and author, and as a sleeping partner in a well-intentioned but unfortunate business with which I became connected in 1926. Finally, I ought perhaps to remark that I am an Englishman who spent many years in Australasia, that I am proud to have served with the Australian Expeditionary Force, and that if real events and persons are sometimes mentioned, they are treated without malice or prejudice on the one hand, and without fear or favour on the other. Except *Felipé*, nobody is drawn-on for a major rôle; other actual persons (there are four or five) merely flit across the stage.

The first three stories, which, slow in movement, form a distinct section, have qualities akin, perhaps, to those of chapters from comprehensive biographies; *A Mere Private* might be described as "a modern chronicle"; *Vernon Ditchley* resembles the stories in the first group, except that the "biographical" flavour is absent; the fifth, sixth, and seventh are not dissimilar, in their treatment of atmosphere and environment, to such a tale as *Jim Dawson*, yet not only do they form a separate group, but they contain much more of straightforward narrative.

C. D.

London, October 1, 1928.

CONTENTS

THE VALLEY

THE VALLEY

THE parents of John Wright were proud of the fact that he was the first white child born in a country district of New Zealand, and it is doubtful whether many Maoris had played their prologue in that deep-set, forest-clad valley of the North Island. Even as a little boy he used to hear of the landing of Captain Cook at Poverty Bay, which, in fact, was not far distant. Although he believed his father implicitly, he could not help wondering why the Maoris should have received the intrepid Englishmen so badly, for all the Maoris that he met were frank and kind ; and when he grew older he was much amused by the curious detail that Poverty Bay was rich of soil and rich in men, while the Bay of Plenty (thus named by the same hero), with a comparatively barren soil, was —he did not see the partial necessity of this consequence—sparsely populated.

Both his father and his mother were fond of him in their very different ways. He was the first-born : and that accounts for much. Later, he chanced to read in his father's diary (if his father had known!) the entry made on the day he was born ; child-like, he felt that this must have been an event of much importance, and he would indeed have been sorely disappointed if he had found no reference to himself. He knew that he was born on a given day and he excitedly turned the pages until he came to the right one. *December the 9th.* (Luckily he had remembered that the year was 1892.)

But the entry itself rather puzzled him. "Edith in grave danger. Delivered of a son. Thank God she is safe!" The boy was slightly piqued that no further notice was taken of him till some months later, when the next volume of the Diary showed a reference to some childish illness; this restored his pride and gave him that feeling of distinction which comes to even sophisticated adults when they see their name in a newspaper or in a book, even if it be only in a footnote.

He passed the first nine years of his life on a farm. But nothing seems to have stood out very clearly until he was five years old, when he went to a party in the small wooden building that was used as church, schoolroom and social hall; amusements were few and therefore all the more impressive when they took place. This party somewhat dazzled him, for he was unaccustomed to so many lights and to such a crowd: there must have been at least thirty persons present. Everyone seemed to be so finely dressed; everyone was smiling. After much talk among the elder people —talk that was above his head, talk of politics or of births, engagements, marriages and deaths (he disliked the last word, though he could have assigned no reason for his uneasiness)—came the real business of the evening. A wonderful Christmas tree was brought from a back room which served the diverse purposes of vestry, teacher's office, refreshment room and dressing room for the ladies at the rare concerts. He had never seen a tree like that, and the first thing he did was to touch the leaves to make sure they were real; it relieved him considerably to find that they were. He soon, however, betook himself to the more congenial activity of walking round and round, admiring the toys and tiny candles, the tinsel and the little stockings that promised so much ; all allured, all tempted him. Yet he did not immediately realise that he was also to share in these good things : the unfamiliar being out of his ken was, of course, out of his reach. His joy on hearing that he was to receive a toy or a stocking, or even (if he were a good boy) both, was so infectious that not only his parents but others standing near offered to choose for him. Very gravely he asked if he might choose for himself ; he accepted the " yes " without questioning the readiness of the reply ; it was not till several years later that he discovered that the reason for this honour was his primacy of birth, a primacy that struck him even then as a strange and inadequate cause of so great an honour. The stockings stirred his curiosity. He looked first at the biggest, but he could see what it contained and rejected it (no one had suggested that he might have it). He finally pointed to a smallish stocking, which held little packets of he knew not what ; he felt that he must learn. A toy train was proposed, but no—his inclinations were not mechanical ; a picture-book, spoken of very highly by his mother, was, after some hesitation, refused ; he looked puzzled until he caught sight of a fair-sized doll, at which he pointed with glowing eyes. His father, annoyed at so unmanly a choice, turned away. Little John held his treasure close and took only a perfunctory interest in the bustle and the games, but showed a proper appreciation when supper was ready ; yet he would not give his mother the doll, which he placed carefully on his lap and guarded jealously from falling crumbs. He ate heartily, although now and again he glanced quickly down to make sure that the doll was still there ; having satisfied himself as to the contents of the stocking, he had yielded it to his father, who went off to deposit it in the capacious pocket of an honest tweed overcoat. On the way home he slept, tightly clutching the doll, which had blue eyes (he thought them pretty though less dark than his mother's) and flaxen hair (quite different from that of any of his relatives).

Next morning, after an early awakening, caused by the delighted anticipation of yet more presents ; after due gratitude for the good things brought to him by Father Christmas, whose entry had been facilitated by the absence of the family at the party ; and after a breakfast smaller than usual, he went out on the verandah with the doll, to show it proudly to several guests. One of these was a boy of perhaps sixteen, fond of games, healthy and heavily contemptuous of girls. Contemptuous also of dolls. John, trustfully offering his, was taken aback by the loud guffaw. " Only girls have dolls! " John knew that he was not a girl and resented the statement, both because he wasn't a girl and because, though a boy, he was passionately fond of the doll. The youth pulled it about while John gazed with increasing anger. Like a little fury, he rushed at the offender and pummelled him with his clenched fists. He demanded the doll, but it was not given him. He raised his voice angrily and shouted : " You horrid man, give me my doll! give me my doll! " Still it was held. After another impotent struggle, the little fellow burst into tears. His mother came out and asked what was the trouble. The guest found it difficult to explain the position and looked shamefacedly away. With tears in his voice, John pointed at the delinquent and said :

" He won't give me back my doll, and he says that only girls have dolls. It isn't true, is it, Mummy ? "

" No, my little man," she replied with a tact equal to her sympathy ; and, turning, she said very quietly but with a hint of disapproval : " Please leave John alone."

She patted her son's head, and he sobbed more quietly ; after a while he asked : " It is a nice doll, isn't it, Mummy ? and no one will tease me about it, not even that horrid man, will he ? "

" No, John," she replied ; " and it's the nicest doll I have ever seen." This comforted him, but he avoided the youth during the rest of the visit.

Gradually, however, the doll lost some of its charm for John, because it did not answer when he spoke to it and asked it questions. He became more interested in his younger brothers, who, by the time he was eight, were companions. But in the interval he had experienced the excitement of a first day at school. He had no fears, partly because he was to go to the hall of that wonderful party, partly because he looked forward to learning to read well. He already knew his letters and he was anxious to find out what really was in the books that his father kept in a small book-case in the dining-room ; the illustrations were familiar, but he wished to know more about them than his father had told him. He rode to school on an old mare named Sally. Sally would stand patiently while he clambered onto her back, the reins resting the while on her neck. At first he did not dare to make her canter, but his father (a good horseman) taught him how to ride properly, though he never came to like trotting; in fact, he would never let Sally trot if he were by himself. He was proud of going to school alone after being accompanied the first week, and he waved his hand to his mother on the first occasion of his independence; she had wept a little, thinking of him setting out thus, and stood on the verandah watching him out of sight. But Sally proving trustworthy, she soon ceased to worry and was sorry when the school was closed down, the response of the countryside being less than had been confidently expected by the local committee.

After some months of lessons at home, given unattractively though efficiently by his father, John went off every morning to be taught by a young married woman whose husband worked an orchard: as it was during the summer and the autumn, the pupil profited by the fruit, which he was as glad to have as his teacher to earn pin-money. Sally carried him, this time in the opposite direction, and safely piloted her rider across the shallow ford of the river. This stream ran the full length of the valley that constituted a district to itself. The Wright homestead was situated in a meadow by the side of this small river, which was yet considerably more than a brook. When John was a baby, it vindicated its rights to be called a river by becoming a flood; a landslide occurred a mile from the house, the water covered the meadow and invaded the house. Henry Wright carried his wife, a visitor carried John, to the woolshed about three hundred yards away and on rather higher ground. Luckily, the spate rapidly subsided. The house remained uninhabitable for a week, during which Henry Wright toiled arduously at the removal of silt, at the sluicing of floors and at the countering of the myriad other spoilings of the inundation. Ever after that, the river remained an object of respectful interest, but, since the flood had been the result of a rare event, not of fear. John and his two brothers went every day in the winter to see how much it had risen; they measured it by certain familiar landmarks and became greatly excited if it reached the ten-feet mark. In the summer they paddled and bathed and, for the most part, forgot that the river could be a foe as well as a friend. Yet they were not allowed to ignore its sinister power, for, when John was perhaps eight years old, an accident startling in its unexpectedness befell a neighbour several miles lower down the river. He was returning from Gisborne, the nearest town, to which he, like Henry Wright and others in the valley, was in the habit of driving with a buggy and pair. On coming to the ford, which was close to his home, he had just entered the water when to his horror he espied an oncoming wall of water (being a Colonial he did not call it an eager) about a hundred yards away. He lashed his horses, got nearly across, and, seeing that he would be unable to clear himself, leapt out; frantically he tried to cut the traces, but, in deadly peril himself, he despairingly abandoned this effort and barely saved his life. Horses and carriage were swept away; the next morning they were found high up on a sharp bend of the river, the former dead, the latter mere wreckage. Perhaps, however, it was the strangeness of this accident, like the remoteness of the flood, which prevented the river from becoming to John a thing of dread; his wholesome respect for it was one of deep affection ; in some ways, he might be said to love it. He played sometimes alone, sometimes with Frank and Tom (Tom, rather delicate, was the youngest) on its banks, and one day he saw his father and mother bathing ; this scene reminded him of Adam and Eve, for he had seen an idyllic engraving of those two in the Garden of Eden in a well-illustrated *Paradise Lost* ; he thought that his mother, perhaps because of her long hair, was very like Eve, but considered his father more handome as he stood glistening in the sun before leading her into the water. Nor did he understand why it was that, on next hearing that his parents were going to bathe, he received an emphatic *No* when he asked his father if he might come to play by the water-side. The picture had charmed him and he felt himself baulked of a legitimate pleasure. But, child-like, he soon forgot his disappointment and turned to more accessible joys. The river, however, remained vivid to him and he was never happier than when venturing to trace its progress for some distance below the house ; the upper part intrigued him less, for the flatness of the meadow carried no trees, whereas, in the other direction, the banks were steep and thickly wooded, the pools were deeper and more beautiful as they gloomed beneath the dark green foliage that here and there was gashed to redness by the flaunting *rata* or whitened by the luxuriant clematis of a bloom much larger and richer than any one sees in England. Perhaps there would be a stretch of swift-running water, or, in the bed of the stream, a drop broken by boulders ; a strip of foam, and then a pool twenty feet deep and some fifty yards across—of such an expanse John was always afraid, and this fear partly occasioned the admiration that he felt for his father when he and his men friends would dive and swim there. The river formed a boundary on one of the two longer sides of the Wright farm, which carried mostly sheep ; though he wished to walk the whole length of the available river-side, John never did so, for it would have taken too long. But he made discoveries that vastly intrigued him, as on the day when he found a patch of mint near the water. (It had been planted there by Henry Wright many years before ; near a piece of flat land which, now covered with a subsidiary orchard, had been originally intended for the house, but abandoned by him on recognising the superiority of the meadow further up the valley.) He took some roots and planted several on the river bank near the house ; several in a brooklet that ran down the hillside and into the river a quarter of a mile away : the former planting came to supply the Wright household, which had previously relied on the patch that John had so gallantly discovered ; the latter was a secret to all save John and his brothers, who visited the brook occasionally to see if the precious mint were still there. This lesser stream afforded the three children a deep pleasure, for they traced it both to its source in a spring far up the hillside and down to its junction with the river. An exploit of merit : they had to creep under branches linked overhead, and climb in places from stone to stone ; never would they depart more than a yard or two from the water : that would have been to fail signally in their rôle of explorers. All three brothers admired explorers. Perhaps their enthusiasm remained at a high pitch because, though the task was arduous and fatiguing, it presented no great danger ; the water was nowhere deep enough to allow them to be drowned, the stones were seldom boulders and the few boulders were well embedded ; moreover, they thought that their father's smile was unalloyed approbation of their achievements. Such activities kept them healthy and happy : and John benefited most of all, for they prevented him from reading overmuch ; there was always some danger that he might become a little bookworm.

Having exhausted the pleasures derivable from the "Mint Creek," John and his brothers passed to the next brooklet, a mere trickle of water this! Not enough to occupy them more than a day or two, yet significant, for the banks were covered with the poisonous *tutu*, against which the children had been warned by their father and which furnished a visiting aunt with a story of unceasing interest, for she and one of her sisters had eaten it as children and been violently ill. The escape from death (actually the simple affair of an emetic) seemed to the listeners to be miraculous after the manner of Daniel's immunity in the lion's den ; the aunt, moreover, was a born narrator, for she varied the story cleverly and embellished it ingeniously. One day, too, a cow ate of the *tutu* and died, a mishap that John compared with the incident of Eve and the apple—an incongruous interpretation that caused his mother to laugh brightly and his father to smother a smile, look reprovingly at his wife, and say : "Don't be silly, John!" It was the death of this, a favourite beast, which set John a-thinking of death and asking his father awkward questions. "Will the cow go to Heaven, Daddy ?"

"No, John, only persons go to Heaven."

"Will it go to Hell, Daddy, for being naughty and eating *tutu*?"

"No, John, I'm afraid it's only persons that go to hell."

"Why don't animals go to either place when they die?"

"Because they do not think and have no souls."

"How do we know that, Daddy?"

"Of course we know, you silly boy!"

"But *how* do we know? Do animals talk?"

"No, they don't talk. But you mustn't ask any more questions: I'm busy, and you're not old enough to understand."

John was silenced but not satisfied, so he asked his mother.

"I'm not clever like your Daddy, John, and I don't know; when you are a big man you will learn more about it."

But although he was to hear much talk about it and about, he never, even when he became a man, *knew* in the real sense of that much-abused word, and he sadly realised that most knowledge consists in an unquestioning acceptance of what others have said or written.

However, after a time of puzzlement, John turned to other things. He continued to explore, by himself or with Frank and Tom. An expedition that often attracted them was a walk to a brook, not far from the abandoned house-site. This stream, cold and pure, ran between high banks for most of its course; a little before it joined the river and at the very boundary of the farm, it rushed down a steep but not perpendicular face of rock. After heavy rains, this declivity became a beautiful waterfall, arboured at its base by tall trees; but in dry weather the water glided, quiet and shallow, almost imperceptibly down the smooth rock and was, indeed, not more than four feet wide : it was at such a time that the boys climbed that stretch of stone, just sufficiently broken to afford them foothold and grasp ; afterwards they descended to bathe in the pool at its base. This limpid pool was not more than three feet deep, thirty feet long, and twenty across, but, as its bed was covered with a species of moss, it looked considerably deeper. After an unusually heavy rain, they went there to see the waterfall, and long would they stand gazing at it. They had heard of Niagara, but Niagara was far away. This was near and it belonged to them.

They were very proud of their ascent of the hill looming high above the house and rising abruptly from the meadow ; it must have been quite eleven hundred feet high, and the latter part of the climb was difficult. When they reached the top, they waved frantically to their mother, who had gone out into the garden to see if she could espy them. After searching the rearward slope awhile for adventure and finding nothing worthy of their metal, they descended to a tea voraciously eaten. It was on the lower part of the hill, and facing the house, that the sheep destined for the house-supply were grazed. It was one of John's keenest pleasures to watch his father stand on the verandah, and, by whistling alone, direct the favourite (because the best) dog to muster the sheep and bring them down to the meadow, the gate between the two paddocks having been opened. The boy did not know which to admire the more, the skill and patience that his father must have exhibited in training the dog and his economy in whistling, or the remarkable intelligence of the animal, for mustering sheep on a steep slope is not an easy task. On this hill, moreover, there grew a number of flax-bushes, in which the children played games and rested ; there, as elsewhere on the farm, grew the even more inviting wild fuchsia, which provides in summer a delicious berry. They knew all about that and waited impatiently each year for " the season " to begin.

But, one day, John met with more than he bargained for. His father took him out to watch the felling of *totara*, *rimu* and *ti* trees in the back paddock ; the two men (for an assistant was necessary in the work of the farm) carried rifles—John wondered why. After lunch, Henry Wright said to his son : " You must stay here on the ridge and not move away. Jim and I are going to shoot wild pigs down in the gully." At first John was happy, watching them descend, but at the sound of shots he suddenly thought : " What if an old boar is only wounded and comes rushing up the slope ? " He had read stories of the fierceness of wounded boars and his vivid imagination drew horrible pictures of a little boy being maimed or even gored to death. He was brave as long as possible, but a yell (it was of triumph at a good shot) made him think that a pig had escaped. Shouting distractedly, he ran further up the ridge to seek a safer place and was just about to climb a tree when his father found him. Henry Wright did not scold ; he contented himself with saying : " You should believe your father, John! You were quite safe," but he was noticeably kinder for some days afterwards to the highly-strung boy, whom Edith Wright comforted more effectually and with a deeper sympathy. The incident threw John more on to his books than usual, until he forgot the unpleasantness and began to romanticise his adventure. He then wrote a brief story on the subject, for at this age of eight he was already infected with the itch for composition.

Several months later, the family went to spend a winter in the town and John became a pupil in a small dame's-school for boys and girls. He and another boy took a fancy to two little girls, sisters, who lived near by and attended the same school. John and his friend, wishing to show clearly to all their rivals that they were the favourites, hit on the plan of parti-coloured hats made of paper and covered with pieces of velvet and satin. They made the hats themselves and took them to the maidens of their choice; the latter, flattered it would seem, added the colours. The boys, at play-time, would don their distinctive head-gear and parade about the yard. But John, not to be outdone even by his friend, wrote a fairy-tale for his Rose and posted it to her, and she, unequal to fiction, relied on the simple truth, protested her undying affection, and promised to marry him when he grew up. When the Wrights returned to the farm, John remembered her. As he feared his father's ridicule, he did not correspond. The dream was shattered when one day Henry Wright drove him to town, for, passing the house where his *fiancée* lived, John saw her playing with another boy. This was in the middle of winter, and, although he had to keep a stiff upper lip and show a manly stoicism as he sat beside his father, he did not recover from this blow to his illusions until the spring was well advanced and the joy of the season led him out once more to the river, the hill-top, and the mint now spreading by the edge of the brooklets. Such scenes and pleasures, he felt, were more enduring and hardly less sweet than those of his first love.

THE SCHOOLDAYS OF TOM WARNER

THE SCHOOLDAYS OF TOM WARNER

TOM WARNER was born in New Zealand, but when he was thirteen his parents migrated to Queensland. Most New Zealanders, if they settle in Australia, go to either Victoria or Queensland ; New South Wales, for some reason or other, is much less popular with them, while the other States rarely see them except as visitors.

There is less transmigration and less travelling between Australia and New Zealand than one might expect. Farming is so different in the two countries that he must be either a brave or a rash man who relinquishes a holding in the one to take up a holding in the other, and the risk is undoubtedly greater for the emigrant to Australia. Moreover, when an Australian goes for a trip he usually visits another State, or if he belongs to the country he visits the capital of his own ; Sydney and Melbourne, indeed, are such fine cities that they attract visitors from all over Australia. If an inhabitant of the North Island of New Zealand leaves his own district for a change of air, he will probably visit the fiords or the mountains of the South Island, while an inhabitant of the latter will as likely as not decide that he should have a look at Rotorua or the Wanganui River. It may, however, be said that, comparatively as well as numerically, a considerably greater number of Tourists cross to the Dominion than to the Commonwealth. There used, between the two countries, to be a certain amount of ill-feeling, which has been effectually dissipated by the Great War; and there is still a wide divergence of character. New Zealanders, whose climate presents no great difference from that of England—one may say that the climate in the South Island resembles that of the southern half of England, while that of the North Island is rather warmer—New Zealanders approximate to Englishmen: English customs and traditions are far more generally and closely observed in New Zealand than in Australia. Australians are more independent, more outspoken, more critical, more iconoclastic, much "harder boiled," more casual, more daring, more picturesque: and they are just a little inclined to consider these characteristics as positive virtues. New Zealanders are quieter in manner, more stolid, in some ways more dependable. These divergences may be traced in part to climate, in part to the life and the men of the early days; to a smaller extent, to the difference in the native races and to the fact that Australia has been, much more than New Zealand, influenced by the United States; and of course to the excessive growth of the city populations in Australia as compared with those in the Dominion. You will find that both Australian and New Zealander are proud of the differentiation, that each loves "the Mother Country" (though the former is shy of admitting his affection), that each has a distinctive (but not, according to Englishmen, a distinguished) accent—which he considers vastly preferable to "the Oxford accent"; that both Australian and New Zealander, when they come to live in England for some time, are slow to assimilate English manners, nuances, opinions, but that when they do begin to do so they are apt to become profound admirers and warm defenders of all that is English : " more English than the English."

It was near the end of the calendar, which in Australasia corresponds with that of the scholastic year, that the Warners migrated. It was agreed that in February, 1907, Tom would go to the local Grammar School at Toowoomba, but as there remained a month before the closing of the schools, he was sent (no doubt to give him something to do, to keep him up to the mark, and perhaps also to get rid of him) to one of the ordinary State schools, that is to say, to a free primary school. It cannot be claimed that he distinguished himself in learning, although he showed himself the best in English in his class. At cricket, however, he shone. Previous to his arrival at school, the game was played with little method and with an almost complete ignorance of the rules. By his enthusiasm and his knowledge, Tom soon wrought a change : at play-time, during the lunch-hour and after school, he was at the pitch with the nucleus of a team. Inter-class matches were played, practice became regular, and, most difficult of all, a subscription was raised to purchase adequate material. Luckily, one of the masters, a cynical bachelor of middle age, was a cricketer playing in a local team ; he willingly acted as treasurer and convener. A meeting was held with all due ceremony, and the business of electing officers took little time. Tom was chosen captain with a flattering unanimity ; an excellent batsman (considerably superior to his chief), the vice-captain. Tom, now regarded with favour by the girls of his class, received button-holes and "glad eyes," but, being both tactful and by no means a girls' boy, he escaped jealousy among his team-mates. After assiduous practice for a fortnight, a match was arranged with another school. The team was accorded permission to depart half an hour before closing time, for the match was to commence at four o'clock in a public park. Tom lost the toss, and the opposing captain elected to bat. The pitch was far from perfect: at one end it consisted of concrete, at the other of virgin soil worn into a slight depression—"a happy hunting ground" for a fast bowler. Runs were made with ease on the concrete, but the other crease saw the downfall of most of the batsmen. Tom put his fast bowler on at the concrete end, and rare damage did he effect, while he himself, bowling from the other, came out with honour and a much worse average. The total runs amounted to 40, of which nearly half were made by the captain, a boy with a good eye and a supple wrist. Yet Tom thought the total was unduly high; he had a shrewd idea that it was little more than 30. He was right in his suspicions, although he did not learn this till later, when he was asked to play in a scratch game in a side led by this same captain: he knew that he had made 10 at the most, and found that his score was 15; remarking on the difference, he was chided severely by the cheat and then, confidentially, informed: "We must win this match." But to return to that in which Tom led his school side. His team went in to bat with no great hopes of winning (it was a one-innings match), since there were only four batsmen that could be trusted to make a few runs; Tom himself was one, withal the least, of these.

Harry Stone, easily the best batsman, hit lustily but survived only one over; out for 7, he had hardly done his bit. One of the other stalwarts covered himself with ignominy by being bowled (it was at the bad end, it is true) by "a regular trimmer" first ball. The champion bowler of the side hit a 4 and succumbed to the next ball. Tom and the last of the dependables added 10 between them (Tom's share being 1); nothing now lay between the side and defeat but Tom and a number of "rabbits." One by one the latter went, though several made a single. Tom kept up his end and remained not out 8, with the side in arrears by nine runs. The defeat was, in its way, decisive, but not overwhelming; honour had not received too severe a blow. Everybody was sympathetic, and in the course of a few days the defeat became, not indeed a victory, but something almost equivalent to a draw. The cricketing master gave Tom some good advice, but he was unable to act on it, for the year ended before another match could be arranged. He left the school content: he ran a good second for the "popularity" prize in his class (the highest), and was assured by several of the nicest girls that he ought to have won it. With these sops to his vanity, he parted on good terms with the very eccentric headmaster, who, interested to hear that he was to go to the grammar school, unbent considerably and, in the process, became agreeably human.

After a pleasant holiday, in which, however, he worked to obtain a scholarship, Tom went to the Grammar School. Without the scholarship: his arithmetic was much too weak; his composition, the best in the whole examination, did not pull him up sufficiently. When he entered the school, it had been established some thirty years, during which it had seen considerable changes of fortune. The Headmaster, a first in "Greats" from Oxford, and the possessor of a delightful English prose style, was an excellent disciplinarian without being in the least a martinet; rarely did he cane more than two pupils in a year. The boys regarded "the head" with profound respect: they almost worshipped his learning, they knew him kind, they dared not omit any ceremony, and they saw that, although he never played "rugger" (for which he was too old), he coached the preparatory school in cricket and was a tolerable golfer, overshadowed, it is true, in this last game by one of the assistant masters, who, representing the State, was rumoured to be, and actually was, its champion, and who was a first-class cricketer and lawn-tennis player. The second master was by no means loved, for he was somewhat too strict; and he was feared for his sharp tongue. When one was older, however, one found that he was "rather a decent sort"; the senior boys almost liked him, while they admired his incisive wit. He was, moreover, unremitting in his efforts to obtain good passes in mathematics, at which he was very able. Two other masters appealed to Tom, who was at times critical despite his innocence. The one was the geography master, who taught also history; a jovial, rubicund, well-meaning and energetic teacher, who played a passable game of cricket and "rugger." The other a general master, in charge of the school cadet-corps; a little tart of tongue occasionally, nevertheless a good fellow, who during the War died heroically in a fruitless and tactically-disgraceful attack, on the Somme, in 1916: a capable teacher, a cultured and amusing man, and a skilful soldier.

The tone of the school, like its position, was healthy; of vice there was none. No scandals, whether sexual or financial, had tarnished its reputation. On the other hand, no mawkishness, no molly-coddling. An ordinarily pleasant lot of boys neither vicious nor goody-goody, and a rather more than ordinarily decent set of masters. A school with as good a name for work as for play, the example being given by the staff so unobtrusively that it was followed by the boys without that reluctance which characterises or even prevents adhesion where an ostentatious display is made of the desiderata. The prefects acted effectually and yet quietly, and very wisely were they chosen; moreover, the headmaster understood the importance of a really impressive initiation-ceremony, which left its mark on the new prefect till he was a very old one or no longer one at all. It is remarkable to what extent those prefects who were initiated during that headmaster's tenure of office (and the same may be said of the present régime) have made their mark, not so much, perhaps, in the highest places as in those posts of responsibility in which loyalty, pluck, and calm efficiency are essential. Like certain other grammar schools in Australia, the Toowoomba Grammar School has formed a tradition and attained to an enviable name: not a shackling nor a retarding tradition, but one which, while conserving what the school has found salutary, admits of development: not a tradition of mere accent or clothes, but of a general bracing attitude towards life, a pleasant camaraderie, an inoffensive self-reliance, cheerful service, manly courtesy. So far as generalisations may be risked, the Grammar School men have not the fascination that dazzles but the agreeable dependability that makes good friends both of and for them ; they exemplify the value of that much-used motto, " a sound mind in a healthy body " ; they are safe, not eccentric, in scholarship ; they are direct, yet in no wise brutal, in business ; they are simple in manner ; just as they tend to common-sense, but not to materialism, in philosophy, so do they prefer the humane in practical, the human in theoretical, morals ; in politics they believe in the value of good local government ; in culture they are neither highbrow nor barbarian, neither very extensive nor cramped, neither fanatic nor insincere.

Not, of course, that Tom thought or knew or felt much of all this when, as a rather shy boy, he entered the school. In science, in mathematics, in formal grammar he was sadly deficient : in the first he did only one year's work, under the care of a man who, though trained in a German university, remained almost startlingly English ; in the second he never attained proficiency, could not or did not remember formulæ for more than a month or two, but was above the average in the solution of problems that required intelligence rather than rules of thumb ; the third remained a stumbling-block until he seriously tackled parsing and analysis, when the difficulties suddenly disappeared and he became truly expert. Those masters who at first rated him soundly for his inferiority in the more " practical " parts of education came to abandon this attitude when they discovered that he was what his fellow-pupils called "hot stuff" in languages, history and geography. At the end of his first year he held an honourable place in the two latter subjects and topped the form in Latin, French and English. When he was promoted at the beginning of the next year, he heard that a special prize in English was being offered, in the higher form, for a paper on a novel by Charles Dickens—a set book in the Sydney Junior examinations. He had read part of it; the paper was to be taken in three weeks' time; he bought another edition, which contained some more than usually helpful notes; read and re-read the story with deep concentration; in fact steeped himself in the book and knew it almost by heart. The test was held on a Saturday morning and he had the good sense not to trouble in the least either about or with the subject before he saw the questions. He answered those requiring notes or comment or paraphrase, to have done with them before giving himself luxuriously to those which called for an intimate knowledge of the book itself; he wrote furiously until he was ordered to surrender his papers. A week later, the results were announced; this new-comer to the form (the only one of a number promoted who thought of taking the paper) headed the list by a clear ten per cent.: he could hardly believe it—nor could the others, who were, however, consoled by the remark that Tom Warner, not having belonged to the form when the competition was first made public, was not properly qualified, and therefore unable to receive the prize. To Tom's credit, it may be added that he did not mind in the least: "glory is enough."

Although he worked hard, he was neither a bookworm nor a prig. He played hard too, and took a normal part in the usual schoolboy pranks ; a formidable hand at a pillow-fight, he organised a raid on the neighbouring dormitory, where tremendous havoc was made of the bed-clothes and occupants. Placed in a small dormitory, he often sent his companions to sleep with interminable yarns made up for the occasion or adapted, rather than adopted, from tales that he had read ; his shorter stories kept them awake. Luckily, one of the boys snored : as soon as he heard this uncomplimentary sound, he snuggled into the pillow and joined the snorer in sleep but not in the heinous accompaniment. Though sometimes asked by the others to tell a yarn, he refused ; on several occasions he was invited—both before and after the raid—to entertain the next dormitory, but he modestly declined ; nevertheless, he felt honoured when now and again several of these boys entered, sat on his and another bed, and listened, thereafter to troop back to their own room. In the summer he played cricket, in the winter " rugger " (though it was always called Rugby at the school). In cricket he progressed considerably : from a poor, he became a tolerable, fielder ; he learnt to develop a useful break in his slow, good-length bowling, which was sometimes hit a little dishearteningly, but which almost invariably obtained a wicket ; in the batting he not only improved on the leg-side, on which he had been very weak, but became proficient at the square and the fine cut and at that very useful stroke, a kind of lob well over the bowler's head, but safely short of an out-field. Both his batting and his bowling possessed a certain amount of guile, for he could hit a very " short " ball for a cleverly run single (having a regular first-wicket partner, he saw that the other was primed), and, when bowling, he varied his speed considerably and would often trick a batsman by running at an ordinary pace to deliver a normal well-pitched ball, which he would follow either with a fast one launched after a tired and casual-looking approach or with a very slow one (having a big break) delivered after a furious run-up ; this last was occasionally the more effective because he might just before have sent down a fast ball after an equally furious run. Another successful ball was that which bumped because it came from an arm that swung almost straight over his head to its full height before it descended with a sudden speeding-up immediately prior to the release ; this he could exploit only in his last summer term, when, aged sixteen, he stood five feet eleven. If his batting was rather staid as a rule, it became determined and forceful when he was set : he did not slog even then, but tried to get the ball away at every stroke, even if it were necessarily defensive. In all departments of the game he profited by attending every cricket-match of note played in the district, and he read the very full accounts of cricketers and games in *The Referee*, a paper in which he considered that the theatrical news was a waste of good paper at the expense of sport.

At Rugby he was not quite so good, for he was lightly built. Nevertheless, he was an indefatigable forward, keeping on the ball, pushing more than his weight in a scrum, clever in a line-out, and a better tackler than most backs. This last qualification caused him to be played sometimes as a three-quarter. As a forward in an inter-form match, he had brought down the most dangerous opposing back just when he appeared to be certain to score; he was moved to the three-quarter line where he proved a success; but so badly was he missed in the van that his captain decided to restore him to his usual position. His brief occupancy of a trusted position in what a friend called "the limelight stage" reminded him of the first occasion on which he had played the game. He was eleven at the time and a pupil at a very large primary school, the oldest boys, those belonging to the newly-opened high-school department, being perhaps fifteen or sixteen; he was only two months recovered from a dangerous illness and had in the interval played no games. He arrived five minutes before school-time; a game of "rugger" was in progress, a tall fellow streaking up the field towards him; impulsively he threw down his bag, dived at the runner's legs, and brought him "a lovely spill." Loud applause. Tom continued to play until the bell rang. After this he regularly joined the class at morning recess and turned up to school-practices among boys ever so much bigger than himself: when he got the ball he passed or kicked immediately, for he had no chance when attacking; but as a defender he excelled, for he could bring down the strongest boy or the fastest runner provided he could find himself within a yard of his passage, for he literally threw himself at the knees—not blindly, but with a keen sense of position —and held on like a limpet; usually the runner came down hard, but if he were particularly big, heavy and strong, he might drag Tom a step or two before those entangling arms caused him to stumble and fall. How that small boy loved a tackle! For several months he lived in a state of pleasurable excitement, dreamed of collaring and put his dreams worthily into action; summer arrived and never afterwards did he recover the zest or the skill of that first careless rapture, which made of his life a kind of exaltation, a high enthusiasm for an idea sustained by a series of exploits no less exhilarating. What high-brows find it difficult to believe is that the thrills and happiness of intellectual pursuits can ever be equalled by the transports of an athlete or a sportsman; that the joy of rhythmic action in running may perhaps rival in intensity the tingle resultant from the creation of verbal rhythm; that the pleasure of a neatly dropped goal, a beautifully made stroke at cricket or lawn-tennis can compete in purity and depth with the pleasure of felicitous composition. It must, however, be admitted that intellectual pursuits have the advantage of being fully accessible much longer than those others: but that is not to lessen the value and the desirability of games and sports, nor to diminish the delight that they give us, for the brain and heart are very differently employed in the latter than in the mental activity, yet they are employed—and beneficially. Tom Warner did not formulate all this, but he sensed it. He would, of course, have been the last to depreciate learning, culture, writing, for it was his ambition "to leave something whereby his memory might last a short day or two before joining the blankness of humanity conglomerated beyond the grave" (to quote from one of his school essays: the subject, *Immortality*), but he disliked those persons who lauded the mental at the expense of the physical, because, as he once declared with boyish dogmatism, "why should not our bodies be considered, not as handicaps, not as our enemies, but as advantages, as our allies ? Our bodies are part of us, we can't be rid of them, they *seem* to be necessary to our life : perhaps they *are* an absolute necessity. Why, then, should we not treat them with honour, get the best out of them ? "

Tom, at the age of sixteen, indeed, was likely to become something of a philosopher : it was, however, the very nature of his beliefs which saved him from the dangers of philosophy ; and he practised what he preached. Moreover, it was contact with life, not reading in books, which set him pondering. During his last year at school he lived with a family in a kind of private boarding house, nearer the town, within ten minutes' walk of the school. The good lady that ran this house would have been deeply offended had one called it a boarding-house, yet she boarded three boys ; she was of the dangerous sort that advertises for "paying guests." Ingratiating towards her superiors, sweet with her equals, and very hard on her inferiors or her juniors ; making a great show of kindness, altruism and generosity, yet possessing a selfish nature, a calculating brain, a spiteful temper ; affable till crossed, and then peeved, sulky ; if resisted in serious matters, sullen and treacherous ; a church-goer who yet insisted that others should go still more ; a seemingly godly woman, who spoke much of religion and held morning prayers, but one who might readily employ mean tricks to obtain her ends and who was certainly a thorough-going hypocrite. She chided Tom for harmless actions and spoke to him as if all boys were not merely imps of Satan but vicious ; she had numerous Spartan rules for the benefit of her three boarders but did herself very well, all the while discoursing on the sacrifices she made. Tom, believing implicitly in the general excellence of women, did not analyse or dissect at first, but he was led to a reconsideration of this illusion when, one Sunday morning, he lay on his bed reading, for he was fatigued after the exceptionally hard game of Rugby played the previous afternoon. She came into the room, glanced at him scornfully, and said : " Tom, you're developing bad habits. Are you not ashamed of yourself ? " (Tom almost felt that he ought to be, and was a little astonished that he was not.) " I don't allow any lying on beds till after two o'clock." Her own son was lounging on his, but apparently she failed to see him (the truth being that she feared him). Injustice more than anything else excites serious thinking ; Tom began in earnest, and it was perhaps due to the fact that he spent, thus, certain hours set apart for study, that, when he sat for the examination at the end of his school-career, he did not obtain quite so good a pass as he might have done. Others considered that a pity : Tom did not, for he had the sense to understand that such things are means, not ends : nor did he for a moment believe that the world would totter to its base if he got five per cent. less than the mark-mongers expected.

JIM DAWSON, TEACHER

JIM DAWSON, TEACHER

At Dalby, in 1909, Jim Dawson began his career as a teacher. Dalby, one ought to explain, is a township of about a thousand persons on the far side of the Darling Downs in Australia. It lies on a plain: an almost wholly pastoral district, with the balance in favour of sheep as compared with cattle. It forms a welcome break in the long journey from Brisbane to the Western part of Queensland, and is itself a junction of some importance, for several other lines terminate there, lines on which three trains run every week in each direction, trains meagrely appointed and most appallingly slow, trains that will stop for almost any reason, trains carrying more of goods than passengers, trains conveying the bread of those within ten miles, the groceries of those within perhaps thirty miles on either side of the line, trains that often transport water in times of severe drought, trains that run past sidings where the task of taking the mail and attending to the railway gates is performed by the wife of a foreman or simple labourer on the line, to termini consisting of townships with perhaps five hundred inhabitants, termini that will in time become stations on the way to further and probably smaller townships as big holdings are cut up on the expiration of government leases. In 1909 there was no high school at Dalby, and of course no grammar school; the State primary school, however, was as good as most and much better than some. The headmaster, though well-spoken, was no great scholar. Yet he knew enough to do his job with a certain bluff ability, and what is more, what is indeed the most important thing of all, he liked his work: children quickly discover when their teacher is bored or indifferent, and they are apt to grow bored or indifferent in their turn: in this difficult profession, enthusiasm and keenness are worth more and give better results than in almost any other, since children thrive on enthusiasm and vivid interest, while indifference results in an apathy that is mental stagnation; and for them stagnation is a tragedy, because it is against their nature.

It was a mixed school, with one other male assistant and a girl just out of the pupil-teacher stage, to which, more or less obviously, Jim belonged, since, at the age of sixteen, he came almost straight from a secondary school. In England a teacher often passes through a diploma-period, or a training-school stage in which he does very little actual teaching (he might well do considerably more) and about the same amount of theoretical work (which might advantageously be less): a period that serves to lessen the shock and gives the incipient teacher leisure in which to realise that no longer is he a care-free pupil or an irresponsible undergraduate: a period that permits of recuperation if he should happen to have worked particularly hard. But in 1909 in Queensland, as at the present time for all except holders of Teachers' Scholarships at the University, there was no such "buffer" stage. And few can guess just how hard can be the first month or two of teaching, especially for a youth in a State school, where all sorts of pupils may be found and where, in fact, a fair proportion consists of those whom at first, he has, to some extent justifiably, no wish to meet but whom he learns to understand, to like and then to improve morally as well as mentally. He has to stomach many features of which he disapproves, sometimes to witness the destruction of pleasant illusions concerning the charming innocence of childhood: innocence among children of the lower classes is rare, and one cannot avoid wondering how much of the world's beauty is lost or dimmed simply because of this precocious knowledge of crime and vice; on the other hand, it says much for human nature that even those whose childhood has been thus blighted will, in favourable circumstances, respond to beauty and goodness. No man, no woman should be allowed to remain a teacher (whether the school be primary or secondary) who has become a cynic. Teaching calls much more for strength of character, for lively and versatile sympathy, for the intriguing presentation of knowledge, than for mere learning.

It must, however, be admitted that Jim Dawson received a severe shock when one day, as he was taking a mixed class whose average age was nine, he saw a paper being passed, amid sniggers, from hand to hand, and when, on demanding it to the consternation of the pupils, he read these words scribbled in pencil on a grubby sheet:

Mrs. Jones will
laundress for men 1/6, *for boys 6d.*

He noticed that, besides the normal creases, there was a marked fold in the paper; that the only letters to the left of this fold were the *la* of that curious distortion of *launder* ; applying the fold, he found himself gazing on that much less innocuous sentence of which the verb is *undress*. The class had hoped that he would read the former sentence only. He thought a moment, but gave no sign of anger until he decided what to do. " Who has seen this paper ? " No reply. Very sternly : " You heard what I said. Who has seen this paper ? " A dozen hands were raised ; five girls and seven boys. " Who had it first and passed it on ? " No reply. But Jim was pretty sure of his ground when he picked on a boy aged eleven, a " re-admission " who, some eighteen months before, had been expelled for a year on a proven charge of sexual misdemeanour (not, be it added, with another member of the school). " You will remain behind at twelve-thirty, Bill Jansen," he said, as he watched the class very carefully ; astonishment indicative of admiration at a shrewd guess and relief that the truth was out showed Jim that he was right. When the class was dismissed for lunch, he allowed Bill Jansen no chance to slip off as he tried to do, gave him a severe talking-to and reduced him to tears ; instead of caning him, he then spoke kindly and pointed out that such behaviour did not make him any more of a man (the boy, being older than those around him, thought he was). Bill certainly behaved much better for several months. But the tare was hardy, as Jim discovered one morning; after staying longer than usual in the class-room to tidy up, he went on to the verandah on his way to lunch at the decent hotel at which he lodged. There he saw Bill Jansen in a corner, laughing and pointing and clearly giving some kind of instruction to two little girls who lay on the floor with their legs extended, their knees raised. The girls, who, aged nine, came from respectable homes, jumped up in confusion and burst into tears as Jim asked quietly: "Aren't you ashamed of yourselves? Shall I speak to your parents?" To the latter question they replied: "Please, sir, don't do that. We are very, very sorry." He reassured them and sent them off home, where they should already have been at lunch. He took Bill back into the school-room, caned him severely and said: "If I have any more trouble from you I shall see that you are expelled." He had no more trouble. He mentioned the matter to the headmaster, who remarked: "It's disgusting that we should have to guard against such incidents, but there you are! That's why one of you teachers is always on duty in the play-ground and why we send the children home straight after school unless a match is being played. I once, when an assistant, was at a school where there was no such supervision, and mightily disturbed we were when we discovered that there were queer goings-on in the play-ground. Yes, in and out of the . . . ahem! conveniences. Deucedly awkward, Dawson; the information came from a widow who had several children at the school. She had found them playing together in an unusual manner and asked them where they had learnt such tricks: 'At school,' they said. She wrote to the headmaster, who immediately begged her to say nothing about the matter to her neighbours, for it was advisable that there should be no scandal: practically every child in the school was mixed up in these 'games.' Luckily none of them were more than thirteen or there might have been a pretty kettle of fish! Good district, too, and respectable homes; in fact nearly all the decent children of the whole countryside were involved. The headmaster addressed the assembled school; said he knew exactly what had been going on—but gave no details; hoped they realised that they had been very silly and that their actions were liable to severe punishment; left it to their sense of fitness. He took the precaution, however, of instituting an unobtrusive supervision, masked by the introduction of organised games in which, at first, a teacher participated; the games were continued, the teacher walked about the play-ground; only the oldest children guessed at the reason of the change, and they were too ashamed to resent the supervision. The headmaster, for his part, considered himself extremely fortunate to get out of it so lightly. As he said to me: 'We have been slack; but, after all, who would have thought that in a place like this, such a thing could have happened!' One cannot be too careful, Dawson, as you see. Luckily we have no such trouble here, but prevention is better, infinitely better than cure in matters of this sort." On Jim's enquiry whether, in the separate schools of cities, this trouble was avoided, the headmaster replied: "In big cities, yes; in towns, not altogether, for the older boys and girls meet after school-hours. God knows what happens!—and it is easy to exaggerate; yet the evil undoubtedly exists and it is extremely difficult to check."

After six months of pupil-teaching, during which he made rapid progress in the elements of the art and learnt the value of variety and surprise in lessons, of firm, watchful and kindly discipline, of a distinguished participation in school games, and of a spotless reputation in one's outside life, Jim accepted the offer of a post at a private school in New South Wales. The township of Scone is small, respectable, and long-established; containing several picturesque ruins, it is one of the oldest inland settlements in Australia. Lying on fairly high ground, it is healthy, and, situated on the main railway line from Sydney to Brisbane, well-placed for pleasure and business. Yet it is too far from Sydney to be much influenced by that gay and bustling capital and it remains very provincial. Life for the better-off is pleasant though somewhat of a backwater; comfortable, agreeable, but far from thrilling. Scone is perhaps the nearest approach in Australia to such a town as Winchester or York: superficially the differences are very great, but, in essentials, the similarity is remarkable. Jim Dawson knew nothing of York or Winchester, but during the six months spent at Scone (April to September, 1910) he came to enjoy the peace of this old township and wondered how it would appear in a Trollope novel; but bickering, intrigue and petty scandal stirred beneath the placid surface. Storms in teacups can be very unpleasant if they indicate more serious trouble in the background. In Scone it behoved one to walk circumspectly, the conventions being strict and touchy: an amusing scene for a man of the world, for a critical observer with a sense of humour, but a little depressing for a youth, impulsive, frank and sincere. The older man either avoids or laughs at the difficulties; the younger becomes entangled in a web of pettiness, although moderate luck will save him from grave inconvenience. If one played "rugger," cricket and tennis, one had a good time, for, all in all, the men were good fellows ; there was also polo for those who could afford it. It was amongst the women that one had to pick one's way carefully, for the place was a hot-bed of gossip ; even those women whose business it should have been to speak well and kindly of all were not averse from slily dropping a venomous word to cloud a hitherto crystal reputation, from putting a malicious and unjustifiable interpretation on an act, from belittling generosity, from twisting an understanding sympathy into a culpable complicity. If one looked at them hard after a particularly atrocious slander, they covered it up by saying : "Of course, I'm only joking." What a life such women must lead! Slandering one another, never knowing what might be said about them in their turn, possessing many acquaintances and few, if any, friends. In townships like Scone, a club or a sewing-guild is a mere excuse to exchange gossip ; a disguised scandal-mart. Perhaps the women are to be pitied : most women love romance, adventure ; in such a place they rarely find it ; frustrated desires, unfulfilled aspirations gradually embitter them ; a nascent romance in the lives of others, or what they imagine to be one (for probably, in actuality, it is an affair as humdrum as their own), excites their envy, so that the disillusioned or the childless wife talks spitefully and puts on incidents an interpretation that could be justified only on the assumption that the person concerned is also married or, at any rate, possessed of an intimate—not a merely haphazard—knowledge that it is rash and perhaps uncharitable to postulate ; so that the spinster abandoned by, or by death deprived of, her *fiancé* or her lover, and the yet more unfortunate woman who has never had either, respectively depreciates what she has lost (depreciates it because of the torturing reminder) and maligns what she would fain experience. This attitude and this atmosphere increase the difficulty and the narrowness of their lives ; emancipation is hard of attainment. If " an old maid "—perhaps a vigorous, healthy woman of forty—were to declare that she would rather be a rich man's mistress than die a virgin, she would be ostracised by such a society ; even the men, sapped by their wives' pettiness, might be vaguely horrified, though they would probably (in secret) admire her courage and admit that such concubinage was no crime.

Jim knew more about the inner lives of those around him than they did themselves, for he was of those men to whom one confides in the sure and certain knowledge that not only does he sympathise but also will he keep a secret without even hinting that he is the guardian of intriguing or perilous confidences. His reliability is its own reward, for he has an enviable insight into life and his friendship is sought and valued.

The boys in the school were not yet infected with the moral miasma ; many indeed came from the outlying districts. They were a clean, agreeable lot, their ages ranging from ten to sixteen. The school, divided into upper and lower, could not have contained more than thirty in all. The headmaster and proprietor was a cleric : it was typical of Scone that its best school was run by a Church of England clergyman. It was not so typical that he was " a thoroughly decent fellow," an able scholar, a tolerable sport, a good disciplinarian and a successful teacher. He was no "slacker," for if he kept his bed in the morning while Jim took "early prep.," he supervised "evening prep.," which lasted rather longer, and thus allowed his assistant an unbroken period in which to study. At breakfast and dinner, the headmaster conducted the meal; at tea (six o'clock), Jim sat at the head of the table in solitary grandeur, though he soon broke the ice by talking with the boys nearest to him, two chairs away on either side.

Not an exciting life. He was glad of the mid-winter holidays and enjoyed the journey through the mountain range, capped with snow where the peaks exceeded 3,000 feet. Bitterly cold they looked in the breaking dawn, and in truth an Englishman would have been surprised at so low a temperature in the Australia of reputedly continuous sweltering heat—in the Australia pictured by certain English novelists.

After a lively holiday in Southern Queensland, he returned to work. He distinguished himself by teaching the boys hockey, which had been introduced at his instigation. But the increasingly humdrum, utterly prosaic life was more than he could stand. He resigned, sat for an examination, and re-entered the Education Department in Queensland, no longer a pupil-teacher but fully recognised. He was sent to St. George, which stands on a plain in the south-west, fifty miles from a railway, on the banks of a considerable stream. Slightly smaller than Dalby and much less important as a centre, St. George was in some respects more interesting. Life there was a little more free, and also a little wilder. Mails from the more important parts arrived four times a week, by way of the South-Western Railway and then from Thallon, or by the

Western line and coach from Yeulba and through Surat. Cobb's Coaches, famous as an institution and still doing good work in this district, were the most attractive means of travelling from the railway line to St. George, and the fifty miles were traversed in surprisingly quick time, the horses being relayed twice, first at a rough hotel which provided very bad meals and very strong drinks, then at a house owned by a small farmer who supplemented his variable earnings from the land with the small but steady allowance made him by Cobb's for the care of the horses. The motor-car run by the same firm from Thallon to St. George is for passengers only and is much more expensive than the coach. Moreover, at this period the driver of the coach was a very amusing man, while he of the motor-car was uninteresting to all save his cronies; the former possessed a fund of stories ranging from the bright to the bawdy, and he told them well, but the other was silent and as dry as the dust that he took a crabbed pleasure in raising. Flat country all the way, save for a few undulations; variety in the soil, which was here a powdery black or brown, there a light-yellow clayey kind of sand; tall gums by the river (which the road skirts but little), stunted gums and either cactus or shrubs elsewhere. Not a very fertile country at the best of times, and a desolate, parched, scorching expanse in a dry summer. Very few dwellings: one ignorant of the district would hardly die of hunger but might very easily walk many miles before meeting with a human being if once the main roads were lost from sight. Jim found it all fascinating, for these plains were quite different from those around Dalby, quite different again from the Darling Downs proper where ranges of wooded hills afford a sharp and pleasant contrast with the plains covered with cereals, lucerne and cattle—cattle stocked for dairy purposes and not, as in the West, for the meat industry. He first drove through it in the motor on a sultry day in February, and being the only passenger he amused himself by opening the gates, for the road was not, for the greater part of the distance, fenced off; it passed through private property, the largest paddock being about ten miles across.

Jim Dawson went straight to the hotel to which a friend had recommended him; he made friends with the old lady who owned it. Full board and lodging cost him the round sum of twenty shillings a week. Arriving on the Saturday night, he went along after dinner to see the headmaster. The next day he wandered about the town, fixing his geography—the school-house, the post office, the nearest store, and the school of arts—a pretentious name that in this case signified a small room containing a library, two tables and a few chairs. The books were few, though some were very good; there was actually a complete set of *The Yellow Book;* one found standard sets of Scott, Dickens and Thackeray, few eighteenth-century novels, only one Gissing, one Trollope, one Macdonald, four Seton Merrimans; on the other hand nearly all Marie Corelli's novels were there (in 1911 that florid writer of the effectively turgid style and the moral shriek was at the height of her fame), just as two or three years later one saw everything written by Maud Diver and Ethel M. Dell; very little verse and a few volumes of essays, but a fair number of memoirs and travel-books; three or four indispensable books of reference—the kind of thing no gentleman should be with; an *Encyclopædia Britannica*; the *Illustrated London News*, *The Strand* and *The Windsor*; the local newspaper, and *The Brisbane Courier*. More than enough—though not much more—to occupy Jim Dawson during the eighteen months that he spent and enjoyed at St. George. Like drifts to like, and he found some congenial spirits. He was rather amused by one of his friends, who, a confirmed reader, received four new novels at the beginning of each month. "How do you choose them?" asked Jim.

"I don't."

"What!" replied Jim.

"I get Gordon and Gotch of Brisbane"—it was in the days when that firm possessed a retail as well as a wholesale business in Australia—"to select them for me."

"Isn't that risky?"

"To some extent, yes; but then they have instructions to send me everything by certain authors." It was in the naming of these that he showed his good taste and his shrewd judgment; his reputation was saved. Not that Jim was a high-brow, for he read almost anything, or rather he tried most authors and rejected them only if they wrote utter rubbish.

The school, built in the shape of a thickly-drawn L, lay only three minutes' leisurely walk from the hotel; the whole town is fairly compact. There were two other assistants, a woman and a youth. The pupils numbered approximately a hundred and forty, the headmaster taking the two highest classes, the girl the youngest children in two classes, Jim two, and the other youth one. Throughout Jim's period there, the completest harmony reigned among the staff, though the headmaster—chiefly because he was a retiring little man, mild of manner, and a better scholar than one normally finds in a primary school—kept pretty much to himself and "interfered" as little as possible. This spirit of amity exercised a happy influence on the general working of the schedule and reacted favourably on the pupils. Jim took part in the cricket played by the older boys, and though he was far from being good, he was the best "all-rounder" among them; the abstention of the other two men from the game (it is doubtful if they had ever handled a bat) strengthened his position. He was liked by the boys and almost worshipped by the girls of his two classes: but then it isn't so very difficult to win the adoration of little girls if one is both kind and firm. They made him presents of flowers, and even the boys showed their affection in touching ways. Knowing that opals were abundant in a district not far distant, Jim once remarked to some boys around him that he would like to obtain a good one; three or four days later, a rather rough lad brought him a beautiful opal and was only with difficulty persuaded to accept a small sum for it. "Look, Tom," he exclaimed, "I wouldn't feel happy about it if I were to take this from you for nothing."

Jim Dawson was often invited to visit the homes of his favourite pupils. (He was not one of that ultra-formal school of teachers who hold that there should be no favourites, and he at least did not "favour" his favourites during hours; jealousy was thus avoided.) He readily accepted the invitations, both to meet the parents of charming or promising or interesting children and to obtain a little social life. He could not dance, and he was debarred (he wouldn't have played even if no prejudice intervened) from gambling ; cards in St. George meant stakes, and usually play ran high before the evening was long in progress. At poker, the usual game among the men, as bridge was in mixed company, one often heard of thirty or forty pounds being lost in an evening, sometimes by those who, on the face of it, could ill afford the loss ; these were probably the best players. Moreover, a large quantity of drink—much more potent than water and much less innocuous than tea or coffee—found its way down those thirsty throats : for all practical purposes, Jim was a teetotaller ; a wise course in these parts, where drink has been the undoing of many weak and some strong men, of mediocrity and talent. One day Jim saw sleeping in the ditch a well-dressed man, obviously dead-drunk and just as obviously meant for better things. He learnt that he was a tutor from an outlying sheep-station, a brilliant Classics honoursman from one of the older English universities who had come out to a good position in Australia, lost it through tippling, and turned to tutoring ; one of a strength of character sufficient to keep him straight for several months at a stretch in the country but insufficient to prevent him from " going on the bust " whenever he came to town ; one conscious of his degradation and keenly ashamed of himself after each drunken bout ; a most entertaining conversationalist, a likable companion. And the cause of his ruin was that old, old cause : his *fiancée*, left in England, jilted him a few months after his departure and just after he had bought a house in Brisbane. There are only too many like him in the colonies, their lives tragic enough but not sufficiently picturesque to furnish the material of so fine and pathetic a novel as *One of the Broken Brigade*, which Jim had read a few days before he encountered this pitiful wreck, but which seems to have become a " back number," forgotten to make way for books vastly inferior. Jim would gladly have done something for him, but did not see how; his regret for his inability was lessened when he heard that several wealthy persons of the district had tried to set him more worthily on his feet only to find that, though the outcast's spirit was willing, his flesh proved all too weak to resist his temptation for long. Most of the drinkers in a place like St. George, however, are either thoroughly seasoned or going the right way to achieve the reputation of being such. The young bloods were harum-scarum, though not altogether feather-brained. Some of their exploits scarcely argued a social *élite* or intellectual worth, but in reality they were little more than the ebullitions of youth. Although it might be reprehensible, it was perhaps humorous and certainly not criminal if, going on the spree, the wealthy young fellows from the stations, allied with a few chosen spirits from the town itself, went singing along the street and lifting gates off their hinges; as a wag remarked in reply to an over-righteous condemnation of such practical jokes: " After all, it isn't everyone who can lift gates off their hinges." They sometimes acted rather childishly as when they flicked a heavily laden table-cloth to the ground and jumped on the crockery; they handed over a cheque for the damages as soon as they regained their mental as well as their physical equilibrium. Sometimes, also, they obviously imitated the American "Far West." An instance? Well, isn't it a patent discipleship in American "manliness" to fire revolvers in an hotel-bar? True, it was at the ceiling of a one-storeyed building, and in mere boisterousness, without the slightest intention of committing bodily harm. These young fellows, in common with most of the others from the bigger stations, spent money freely, played an excellent game of polo, and, once or twice a year, visited either Brisbane or Sydney, where they acted with courtesy and charm and where they were (as financially they might well be) regarded as desirable "catches"; it may be added that they usually enjoyed themselves very thoroughly before they were "caught." A class that it were easy to belittle, a class that, on the other hand, has many good points. They know pretty well all there is to be known of the pastoral life, they love the land, and they are fit and healthy, skilful at games, proud, independent, courageous and good to have by one's side in a tight corner; they possess *savoir faire* and are at home in the city. In time of war, they volunteer readily and make excellent soldiers, as the public discovered (as if they hadn't known at the time of the Boer War!) during the European War, when they mostly joined the Light Horse; those few who enlisted with the infantry, air-force or artillery were fine fellows, excelling in reconnaissance work, in observing, and in sniping.

Jim saw a little of them at fairly close quarters but did not mix with them: he had neither the money nor the slightest inclination. He played cricket in the summer, tennis in the autumn, winter and spring. One of his friends was captain of a local tennis club, which possessed a good hard court and a practice court made by removing the grass, levelling, rolling and watering; nobody played by choice on the latter, for the advantage went with the server even more uniformly than it appears to do in first-class tennis (for that at St. George was hardly more than "pat-ball"), and the bounce, although it afforded excellent training in adaptability and rapid change of position, was a snare and a delusion to the innocent. Jim was amused by the embarrassments of captaincy related to him by his friend, who spoke sarcastically of the most dreadful of the "rabbits": "In general, old man," he said, "the worst players in a club are the most difficult to satisfy; they seem to think that they have a right to play more often than anyone else, and are quite indignant if at least once in the afternoon they are not paired with the best player. Some of the girls want always to be partnered by the man on whom they have their eye, while others refuse to play with a certain male—investigation yields the information that it's a former *fiancé* or a former lover; some sniff when in a ladies' four they are asked to partner so-and-so, than whom they consider themselves infinitely better either socially or at tennis. In fact, to be a good captain of a tennis club, one should know not only all the past history, but all the current gossip. I am not sure that a knowledge of the future would not also be useful." He paused. "And look at my own position with regard to games, Jim!" he burst out. "If I play with the leading players and thus make an even four, I'm accused of giving myself the best games ; the women appear to think that I should take part only in mixed sets—and you know that there are precious few women here who really could tell the difference between a tennis ball and an apple. Thank heaven, this business comes only on a Saturday afternoon! " During the week, these two played singles in the late afternoon, except in June and July ; and Sunday morning often saw them at it. The club did not meet on Sunday afternoon, though some of the graceless turned up occasionally for a game. The members belonged to the respectable part of the population, indeed to the more stable portion of that part, and general Sunday tennis was condemned, as a very virtuous dame scathingly informed Jim, who, smiling in his most disarming manner, asked gravely : " Do you think, Mrs. White, that people who play tennis on Sundays will go to hell ? "

" Oh, I wouldn't say that! but I don't consider it quite nice."

" A little immoral, Mrs. White ? "

" Oh, no! not immoral."

" Bad manners, perhaps ? "

An impatient shrug greeted this sally. " Well," Jim persisted, " do you mean that 'the best people' don't do it ? " She knew very well that it was precisely " the best people " who did it most. " I believe," resumed Jim, " that your disapproval comes to this : You consider I ought not to play, merely to avoid hurting the feelings of those who (for some vague reason or other or, more probably, from mere undefined prejudice) think I shouldn't play."

" You're too clever for me," she exclaimed spitefully, " but I know what I think."

"Then why don't you tell me, Mrs. White? You won't hurt my feelings, and you know that I listen to your opinions with respect." This last statement was an exaggeration, but it left the good lady stranded: she was unable to accept a cordial invitation that flattered her, unable to justify the implied praise. "How stupid I am," she thought; she had not the honesty to admit that she was incapable of proving Jim wrong. After that, she said nothing about Sunday tennis and fought shy of discussions, but she satisfied her pique by saying nasty things about him behind his back. These little victories over women are too dearly bought. It is better to let them keep their prejudices intact, unless one can afford to ignore the harm that many wreak—or unless one does not care a damn what they do.

Apart from tennis and cricket, Jim took but a modest share in the general social life; on the special occasions, however, he "did his bit"; he went to all the parties and concerts. Sometimes he was invited out to the stations on Sunday, and there he had his first experience of eating under a mosquito net. The flies were pretty bad. This never happened to him at St. George itself, and he had no desire to repeat the operation, for flies are worst in the hottest weather and a mosquito net shuts out some of the badly needed air.

He was sorry to leave, although the departure was his own choice. He had decided to work for a University scholarship. In due course, after three months of concentrated study in Brisbane, he sat for the examination and was tolerably satisfied with his papers. A scholarship was his, for he wasn't altogether a blithering idiot (as one friend elegantly remarked to another). Badly needing money, he taught for five weeks, until the University session began in mid-March. This time in a small private school, not unlike that at Scone, but with a younger set of pupils.

While there, Jim read that future classic of schoolboy life, *Pip*. The portion dealing with school struck him as being particularly vivid, true, and sympathetic towards both masters and pupils; crammed, too, with laughter. He amused himself by comparing it with *Tom Brown's Schooldays* and with *The Hill*, both of which he liked immensely. Hughes's masterpiece was the second book he had ever read (the first being *Robinson Crusoe*), and he well remembered that he had been as bored by the descriptive commencement as stirred and excited by the rest of the book. *The Hill* he read as a boy, soon after it was published: he had enjoyed it from beginning to end. What matters it if Harrovians find it "no true picture"? It is the book by which its author may live; not great, but moving work. The comparison led him on to reviewing the other school-stories he had read. Among these, his favourites were the tales of Harold Avery and Talbot Baines Reed; he slightly preferred the latter. Good healthy stuff! Amusing too.

It was a pleasant school in which to live and teach. The headmaster was "one of the best"; manly, capable, an admirable teacher, an exceptionally versatile player of games; sympathetic with the boys, a companion to the two assistants. Jim's "stable companion," as he called himself, was a good teacher and disciplinarian, but a "queer fish," as others called him; he lost his job after four months' tenure of it, for, poor fellow, he loved too well the wine that is red and the beer that is brown. Jim could have remained as long as he wished, but, naturally, he passed on to the University.

Late in his first year, he again found himself very short of money, not because of extravagance, unless we consider that liberal purchases of books to help him in his work were an extravagance. So he sought to add to his meagre allowance of fifty-two pounds a year. For six weeks, thanks to a special intercession of the powers that be, he taught at the largest grammar school in the city; one of the masters had fallen ill. This was a more severe test of his abilities, but he came out of it with credit and a useful sum in ready cash.

The War arrived. Jim enlisted early—and saw much. His next experience of teaching came many years later. A big change, for it was at a secondary school in the South of England. With several degrees to his name, he was well qualified in the matter of learning, but it took him some time to accustom himself to the different ordering of school life, and he thanked his stars that it was a day-school. Day-schools allow one to adjust oneself the more easily, for errors do not pursue one after teaching hours. He began in the winter, but did not supervise the games of "soccer," for he knew nothing about that variety of football; nor was hockey played. When the summer months came, he pulled his weight by an enthusiastic refereeing of cricket matches in the lower school. And he did much to further the game in his own form. He liked his work as a history and geography master, and it was with pleasant feelings that he left the school to take up a better post elsewhere. Yet the incident that he recalls with the most amusement was not particularly flattering at the time of its occurrence. When doing geography with a junior form (not his own, where such a thing could hardly have happened) he noticed that a boy in a corner was drawing. Now drawing was distinctly uncalled-for: the pupil should have been listening, or at any rate looking as if he were. Jim walked quietly over to the inattentive one, put his hand on the paper, and said: "I suppose this is for me, Wilkins?" Wilkins, aged ten, started violently, turned pale, then red. Jim took up the paper, a sheet of foolscap containing script and sketches. It very definitely was for him, as a glance soon proved. "A valuable and most interesting document, Wilkins. All your own work?"

"Yes, sir," replied the frightened boy, as a few of his neighbours gazed at him and wondered what dreadful fate would overtake him; three or four had been privileged to read the sections as they were completed. "You will come to see me at four o'clock, Wilkins; room No. 10." When he had more leisure, he studied the libel very carefully, with mingled feelings of indignation, surprise, anger and admiration. "James Dawson as a baby," was the first section: a ridiculous baby at that. "Our Jim thinks he can sing like Peter Dawson because he has the same surname," he read beneath the sketch of a tiny boy blowing out his cheeks in a perfectly monstrous fashion. "Jim serenades his first love," came next: he was apparently about nine years old, standing in a garden and singing to a little girl leaning out of a window on the ground floor of an unflatteringly small house. The fourth showed him as an earnest student, with piles of books on a table before him as he sat with his head propped by one hand. In the fifth he appeared to be a spectator of the signing of Magna Charta: just a week before, Jim had given a graphic account, couched in the historic present, of this event; he had told it so dramatically that one little fellow, absolutely swept away, exclaimed: "Were you there, sir?" to the general delight, which Jim had robbed of its sting by saying "No, Colton, but I would like to have been there as a baron, with you as my attendant page." In the last, he was represented as an explorer excitedly waving a flag on the top of Mt. Everest. The closing paragraph (for when Jim caught him, Wilkins was adding a few touches to the sketches, *finis* figuring already at the foot of the sheet) consisted of the words: "Mr. Dawson, our dearly beloved teacher, has a wonderful future behind him. Perhaps he will receive a medal for his doughty deeds—of the tongue. Let him rest in pieces." As Jim felt, it was not the work of a generous, high-spirited boy; not of an altogether nice boy. But devilishly clever for his age. At four, Wilkins came in quietly. Jim purposely kept him waiting several minutes after glancing at him. "Would you like the headmaster to deal with you, Wilkins?"

"No, sir, please!"

"Are you proud of this performance?"

"No, sir."

"Why did you do it? You have no reason to bear me a grudge; you have never been unjustly punished."

"It was to amuse my friends, sir."

"I trust that your efforts were successful, Wilkins."

Rather hesitatingly: "Ye-es, I believe so, sir!"

"Do you think that it was fair to me, to show that sheet to them?"

Understanding shone in his eyes; he blushed, then: "No, sir, it was a mean trick, but I didn't think of that at the time."

"You were so pleased with your drawing and composition?"

"Yes, sir."

"Do you think it was a nice thing to do, even if you were not going to show it to anyone at all? I mean, do you think it was kind to me or worthy of you?"

"Oh, no! sir."

"Would you do that to your father, Wilkins?"

Pained, but with a look that indicated his appreciation of the master's point of view: "No, sir, I wouldn't."

"Because you would be afraid of a beating?"

"No, sir; because it would be a horrid thing to do."

"But isn't what you've done here, horrid?"

With tears in his eyes: "Yes, sir, and I'm awfully sorry."

Jim laid his hand a moment on the downbent head: "All right, laddie, you may go."

The boy looked at him gratefully, tried to say something, choked, and ran hastily away.

A MERE PRIVATE

A MERE PRIVATE

I

EGYPT AND GALLIPOLI

When War broke out, Harry Onslow was under age; working in a solicitor's office in Brisbane. He proceeded to his intermediate examination in law. Private affairs occupied him until April, 1915, but so soon as these were settled he decided to enlist. Nor did he allow the decision to grow cold. He walked up to the Victoria Barracks, passed the inadequate and perfunctory tests, and was instructed to report at an infantry camp at Enoggera three days later. On April 24th he duly presented himself at the camp, which, conducted with a show of military efficiency and discipline, was, in sober truth, very slack. Physical exercises before breakfast, drill in the morning, and, though less, drill again in the afternoon. Kit and equipment were served out only a week before the departure. Harry had been in camp precisely four weeks when he left with the battalion.

They camped for some days in the Show Grounds at Sydney. Leave was granted freely; he profited by this opportunity to make himself better acquainted with the liveliest, largest and most modern city south of the Equator. He visited the Art Gallery, wandered about the Domain, called on a friend on the North Shore. Twice he went on excursions round that magnificent, that lovely harbour—the most beautiful in the world, as Sydneyites carefully impress on all visitors : " our 'arbour " is by them applied as an irritant to the sore place of Melbournites, " the stinking Yarra " : these contrasted features are dragged by the Sydneyites into all the numerous debates and recriminations between the two populations, which are divided by a rivalry so keen that they almost become opposing factions. The outsider ends by finding this exchange of amenities both wearisome and crude.

Each city, too, boasts of the greater difficulty and picturesqueness of its native slang-code, which must not be thought of as the general Australian slang slightly modified by the local conditions : these two slang-codes are spoken in the lowest strata of society and are as incomprehensible to the decent Australian as " thieves' language " to the corresponding Londoner. Australians who have no stake in the matter agree in recognising the marked superiority of Sydney and Melbourne over the other capitals. Melbourne, the better laid-out city, is likely to appeal to Englishmen more than Sydney does ; it is the more solid, both socially and financially ; it is more dignified and calm. The average educated person would probably prefer a holiday in Sydney, residence in Melbourne. In art and literature, Melbourne is the more puritanical —the more philistine, but one feels that it is also the more sure in matters of taste ; small cliques merely exist in Melbourne, whereas they flourish in Sydney. One can perhaps sum up by saying that there is more of movement in Sydney, the greater stability and strength in Melbourne.

The other capitals strike one, in comparison, as just a little provincial. Brisbane is in a state of social and commercial flux, which may result in a continuance of its recent rapid growth, but which may also end in a stunting of its potentialities. Its intellectual life has progressed in a most pleasing manner since the opening of the University, but the genuinely cultured are still seen to be in a startling minority if set side by side with that proportion of the population which by its education and financial position could, but seems to have no wish to, advance beyond mediocrity. Adelaide, on the other hand, is, proportionately, the most cultured city in Australia; in this respect, and in the general outward appearance, it is the Commonwealth's only approximation to Oxford or Cambridge. In Adelaide, Government House and University have a delightfully old-world look. Adelaide escapes the nondescript, sometimes degrading influence that so often results when a big city is a mere continuation of its port, and it furnishes much the best Australian example of wise town-planning, for about the central business area is a ring of park-land, beyond which lie the residential suburbs. Perth boasts a pleasant river and a pretty park, but it is at present little more than a glorified country-town: its buildings are low, its streets and footpaths much too narrow. There is an air of "Damn you! I'm as good as you are if not better!" about the place; independence becomes a rather crass self-assertion; culture is at a discount, the spirit of propaganda informing almost every phase of society. Examine the attitude of this capital towards its intellectual *élite* and you will start back when you learn it. Perth needs mellowing, and only time will fulfil that desideratum. It is a city that has so far made little of its potentialities. There has been much more of real progress in

Hobart. It is, however, doubtful if a native of any other part of the British Empire could differentiate between the inhabitants of the various Australian capitals, and no English visitor has yet succeeded in giving a satisfactory or even a rhetorical account of the various cultures and " atmospheres," which are becoming more and more sharply distinguished. Of the earlier travellers, R. H. Horne, whose *Australian Facts and Fancies* Harry had picked up at a second-hand book shop in Brisbane just before he left, comes the nearest to divining Australian needs and to understanding the Australian character, and of the post-war observers from abroad no one has surpassed D. H. Lawrence in realistic picturesqueness. Unfortunately, there is at present no native novelist to do for the Australia of to-day what " Rolf Boldrewood " did for that of his generation ; and no twentieth-century writer of sketches has equalled Henry Lawson. But after a " dead season " comes a time of activity, and perhaps we shall in the fourth decade of this century see Australian literature experience a renaissance.

Some of these thoughts were Harry Onslow's. He had received an excellent general education before he was put to the Law, and his profound interest in men and things was to widen and become enriched in the next four years. The army itself was a source of benefit, for he had kept a little too much to himself before he entered it ; his knowledge of society (in the broadest sense) was a trifle limited. He knew this, and such a consciousness of his shortcomings was the determining factor in his maintained decision to go through the war, providing always that he had the good luck to survive, as a private. It is true that he was once a lance-corporal for five days, but this was due to the fact that his section was without a leader in the attack planned for the end of that period: a sense of duty urged him to yield to the instances of those about him. But when he was wounded and sent away, he relinquished that promotion and, on returning to the battalion, he refused to retain his lance-corporalship. He also resisted the pleading of his parents, who would have liked to see him an officer. He felt, too, that his cherished independence was safer when he was a private; in a measure he was right. He was more free to observe his fellows, to wander about, and to read, for whenever he could, and had nothing more exciting to do, he read widely.

At the end of that pleasant and well-filled week in Sydney, the battalion rejoined the ship. They marched to it by way of the rough suburb known as Woolloomooloo (the name figures frequently at Australian spelling-bees). Harry was amused by the sublime tactlessness displayed by a wrinkled, kindly old woman, who called loudly to the passing troops: "I *do* hope you poor boys won't get killed!" The gloomy thought was forgiven in one who so obviously meant well; and in any case death seemed a far-off, unreal contingency at that stage of active service, the cheering and the shouting a near, almost tangible reality.

The ship went straight from Sydney to Port Adelaide, where it stayed only long enough for three hundred South Australians to embark amid those stirring, pathetic, humorous incidents which characterise the departure of a troop-ship in the early days of a war. Later, when the soldiers and their relatives and friends know that it might easily be the last time they will meet, the scene has very much less humour and more of quiet tragedy. But the departure from the wharf is always a fine sight, let the croakers say what they will. The overtones and undermeanings of such a scene ought surely, instead of destroying its beauty and significance, to heighten them.

The crossing of the Bight proved calm. At Fremantle they stopped for a day to ship vegetables and to give the men a turn on shore; a brisk march beyond the town in the morning fatigued most of them sufficiently to keep them aboard in the afternoon. The dispensation of the military may be dull, but it is shrewd and, if one takes the long view, kindly in its prosaic way—and after all the prosaic is good enough for nine men out of ten. The others suffer and reflect; mentally and morally tortured, they yet endure; they act with a courage that produces the same result as the unreflective gallantry of the hard-headed and humdrum. To claim that this choice minority make better private soldiers and non-commissioned officers than the majority would be to render the truth a disservice; it is also doubtful if they make better lieutenants. Only in those ranks where intelligence should be regarded as a *sine qua non* but is so often lacking is that minority superior. But as men they are superior always and everywhere, and after they have been tested in the furnace of war—tried on genuine active service, not merely rendered slightly uncomfortable in some "cushy" job at home or at a base in France or elsewhere—either they are nervous wrecks who, however, pull themselves together at a pinch, or they have become the very salt of the earth. Already several English writers have produced work that, in its general effect, owes to their war-experience its biting sincerity, its quiet realism, its divination of and sympathy with suffering, its contempt for sham and cant. Men like Forster and Mottram and Herbert Read have, at their best, succeeded also in presenting actual war-pieces that may be compared with those of Zola, Tolstoi, Barbusse, and are far superior to those in *The Four Horsemen of the Apocalypse.* Such writing has naturally been praised most by those who have suffered, but so much of universality has come to the writers through pain and stress of thought that their work appeals, or should appeal, to all except the jelly-fish, the barnacle, the shark and the octopus.

The close-packed life of the transport served to bring the men into closer contact than that effected by a camp. All sorts and conditions, with their civil peculiarities not yet smoothed into military uniformity, drilled and ate, rested and slept, bathed and walked in the best variation of the communal life. They were not so crowded as to prevent the formation of groups; like sought, and responded to the attraction of, like; circles formed, diminished or increased, broke up or, if large, became a general bond of camaraderie, if small an intimate knot of four or five; instead of "the eternal triangle," one found a much more attractive union between three men; and pairs of friends cemented their former affection or gradually, after a commencement often fortuitous, built up their friendship. Harry Onslow himself possessed an old and good friend in Don Wall; aboard and in Egypt, they saw much of each other, and continued to do so as long as circumstances permitted (they were not in the same company), yet even on the transport there germinated a closer friendship between Don Wall and a cultured, upright, intelligent young Englishman, and in September of the same year (1915) Harry Onslow became the best friend, and made the best friend, of Jack Phillips, to whom he had scarcely ever spoken and then only in the way of routine, but whom he had particularly noticed very soon after leaving Port Adelaide, for he seemed to dominate the men two tables further aft with a superiority at once physical and mental, at once of experience and ingenuity.

It was a long run without a port of call, from Fremantle to Port Suez. The tropical heat was borne cheerfully, tempers remained equable. Canvas air-chutes prevented the holds, in which the men ate and slept, from becoming unbearable; many slept on deck, but Harry, who had the gift of biding his time and making himself comfortable, stayed below, retained his hammock, and secured a position every night close to a port-hole: the moment hammocks were obtainable from the bins, he was there to claim his; and after a night or two his position was recognised. One soldier never jumps another's "possie." Such facts delighted Harry, who, though independent and no "mother's white-haired boy," had been delicately nurtured and had expected that the discomfort, the material unpleasantness, and the roughness of his fellow-soldiers would be much greater than, actually, they ever were during his long and various service. He studied those about him, talked little but listened attentively to the conversation and yarns of the persons and groups near him, and read often. Many had books, none had more than half-a-dozen.

Exchange was frequent not only between friends and acquaintances but between complete strangers. Harry re-read Tennyson's *Works* and a number of Shakespeare's plays, lent him by Don Wall; Chateaubriand's *Atala*, *René*, and *Dernier Abencérage* in a single volume bought in Sydney, where he had at the same time purchased a charming selection from Victor Hugo's lyrics, prefaced with an exquisite study of the great poet's lyricism ; Meredith's *Beauchamp's Career*, wherein he chafed to find several pages missing ; Kalidasa's *Shakuntala* in Everyman's Library—his first experience of native Orientalism, which he much preferred to Hugo's *Orientales* and to Bain's pastiches, both encountered several years earlier, when he dreamt not of war ; *The Old Curiosity Shop* and *The Yellowplush Papers* ; and lighter novels, by Boothby, Oppenheim, and James Payn. A queer mixture! But in such circumstances one reads what one can, not altogether what one would take down from the shelves of a well-equipped library. If confirmed readers had often to content themselves with inferior matter, it is also certain that the war set reading many a man that otherwise might have never opened a book.

Unobtrusively, Harry took a keen interest throughout the War in the reading of those about him. Late in 1916, he was in an isolation camp—someone, luckily, had contracted measles—at Etaples. He was with a pleasant tentful, they knew they were to be there a month ; so, early in the first week, they clubbed together to obtain some books. Harry had the lists of the Home University Library and Everyman's Library with him, suggested titles, and sent off to Hatchard's for the books. They arrived with only a slight delay, these ten volumes, which ranged from novels to *A History of Scotland* and *A History of Nonconformity*. Each read the book of his choice and then, as the volumes became available, passed on to something else; nobody fared too badly, for one of the rules of selection had been that no book was to be purchased unless three of the men approved; four of the books had received the votes of all, and even the *Nonconformity* had five readers.

The battalion disembarked at Port Suez and proceeded by train to Cairo, whence they marched to the huts awaiting them a mile from Heliopolis. There was a long line of these huts; high and airy, they served as mess-rooms, halls of instruction, places of recreation. Parallel thereto, a line of tents, four or five deep. There the battalion remained from the middle of July until early September. At a quarter to five, reveille, at a quarter past, a light snack and coffee; at a quarter to six, the fall-in, and at six began exercises, drill and route-marches, which lasted till nine o'clock. The route-marches in the neighbourhood of Heliopolis were preferred to the monotonous platoon and company drill; for some reason or other (probably the convenience of the senior Australian officers and the English staff officers), battalion and brigade movements were reserved for the evening period. At half past nine, breakfast proper; from ten-thirty till noon, verbal instruction "at the easy" in the huts; at twelve-thirty, dinner as it was called. Until four o'clock, one could do as one liked: mostly one slept. A kind of afternoon tea was served by the orderlies at four-thirty, and from five till seven-thirty, sometimes until eight, one drilled again. Occasionally this uninspiring routine was varied with a course on the rifle-range or competitions in message-passing, distance-judging and the like. Four times there were night-manœuvres in the barren hills or trench-digging in the desert, the latter an all-night affair rendered memorable by the coming of the dawn. Against the contiguous hills, the clear first lights glistened with something of the world's pristine glory ; a cool breeze refreshed the weary men. Harry recalled the wonder of the sunrise and sunset in the Red Sea, especially a fall of day just past the Straits of Bab-el-Mandeb, when the high, gaunt ranges on the left were bathed in gold, orange and yellow, darkening to auburn and a strange bluish green ; the toughest of the "hard boiled" gamblers and loungers stopped awhile to regard a scene at the like of which they had never gazed before, and all voices were hushed ; cursing and swearing, blasphemy and obscenity shrank back, shamed and confuted. The power of utter beauty had wrought more than the most stirring preacher, the most eloquent orator could have done. "Perhaps," thought Harry, "this is true religion, into which controversy dare not intrude. Roman Catholicism and the Established Church, Nonconformity and the Exotic Sects, even Agnosticism and Atheism recognise something divine ; yet if to some of these men one were to suggest divinity, they would immediately curse and revile again." (One might add that he himself tended towards agnosticism, but not of the carping, hair-splitting kind.)

He had further chances of observing the reverence excited by beauty in nature when he went to Gallipoli. In September and October the men would look across to Mudros and watch the play of the declining sun on, then behind, and, at the last, apparently from beneath the two islands. Across the bay the long lights stretched from shore to shore: silver and golden pathways stood out, sharp and lovely, from the darker water on either side: the crest of the islands seemed at once detached from, and fused with, the sun setting just above them, the strip of golden light grew narrower and slowly disappeared, the perimeter of both magic isles now formed a lustrous halo restricted in width but marked by a rapid gradation of hues, and, as this aureole dimmed and the sun sank level with the sea, those two masses of land appeared to rise from a sheet of dark flame: then as that dazzling whiteness which lies at the heart of light fled silently when the sun dipped, orange and purple, mauve and opal green flickered a moment on the waters and gave body to Mudros and her sister isle; these hues lost their brilliance, yielding to pearly grey and hazel brown and softened black, a luminous band flickered a moment on the sky-line, night fell, and the men on the slopes awoke from their trance.

Leave was given to Heliopolis and Cairo. To the latter, Harry went sometimes with Don Wall, sometimes by himself. He dutifully visited the chief "sights," but what intrigued him most was the native quarter, through which it was advisable to wander in company. Quaint trades plied by the Egyptians; the primitiveness, callousness, and shamelessness of native life; the varieties of architecture, from mosque to squalid hovel, from pretentious café to humble stall; handsome men, men that looked like beasts, hideous old women and pretty girls—many of whom were either already, or perfectly and immediately willing to become prostitutes, children strangely beautiful or prematurely blighted; life at its noisiest, most ribald, most various, where suffering rubbed elbows with joy, disease displayed its horror and animal health flaunted its strength, filth encumbered the ground and loveliness waved in a tapestry; where obscenity was so patent that it seemed a nightmare, an impossibility; where thieving and whoring flourished at all hours, barter was always in season, and murder stalked abroad at night. A place that fascinated even while it repelled. The European part of Cairo has charm and beauty, but it is most interesting where most cosmopolitan: in those few cafés and restaurants which are frequented by Europeans, wealthy Egyptians, and aristocratic Arabs. Heliopolis on the other hand is as small as it is artificial, for naught but the whim of a European monarch here turned a village into a resort, the popularity of which, by the way, has been seriously impaired by the War. Harry on several occasions was sent in the early morning into Heliopolis or Cairo on small commissions for the company orderly-room. He liked to watch the natives early at work, to stroll through Cairo when there was much business afoot but little pleasure, when the air was still cool and fresh; as the big cafés would not be open, he slipped into some small native shop to drink a glass of syrup or a cup of coffee, and to eat one of those curious honey-cakes, but he had the sense to keep to what looked safe; to offset this, he would sometimes, if he were on leave in the late afternoon, go to the largest café, famed for its pastry and cakes. Shepherd's Hotel had long been declared out of bounds to all under commissioned rank, but such restrictions as this did not ruffle him, for he accepted the penalties along with the privileges of being a mere private.

At last, preparations were made for Gallipoli. Everyone desired to go, and soon, everyone regretted that he had not been at the landing there, for friends had distinguished themselves in an exploit that, for sheer audacity, was hardly ever equalled and certainly never surpassed during the whole course of the War. Such regret only steeled them to do their best when they should arrive. They entrained for Cairo ; it was a most uncomfortable journey in horse-trucks ; *wagon pour* 8 *chevaux ou* 40 *hommes* became one of the soldiers' stock jokes. But the discomfort was forgotten as they passed through the Delta in the early morning and the level rays of the sun glinted on water and reed. The troop-ship was small ; the men had little more than elbow-room. Danger lurked in the sea, German submarines were active. The transport before theirs had been sunk, yet all were rescued by a cruiser and a destroyer. The food was good and plentiful : " pigeons fattened for killing," remarked a pessimist. The officers held frequent inspections of equipment and rations ; water bottles were filled and examined on the afternoon prior to disembarkation.

It was mid-way between Alexandria and Anzac Cove that Harry " met " Jack Phillips, shortly to be addressed always by the name of Felipé. He was reading Omar Khayyám, when Phillips looked across the equipment that he was putting in order and said : " I wonder what the old boy would have thought of the present situation ? He might have made a good quarter-master sergeant. *Turn down the glass . . .*" and, having completed the quatrain, " I'd like a loan of your Omar when you've finished."

" I'm re-reading it myself. I'll give it to you as soon as I've done with it."

They talked for some time about Omar. Now, as others have found, conversation on this subject leads naturally to talk " of many things," less of cabbages than kings, and less of either than of one's experiences and impressions. Phillips spoke picturesquely, vigorously, and spontaneously; he possessed wit and humour; he had a mind at once penetrating and comprehensive; and in an irregular way he was well-read. He had travelled much, observed closely, fended for himself both in various grades of society and where society was an empty name, a rumour of a thing unreal. Harry's travelling was slight, his knowledge of life small; but he also was a keen observer; he had read widely; he spoke well; and his friends admitted that he had a mind of his own, was " all there " and was neither prig nor prude. These two, in short, became firm friends the moment they exchanged thoughts, notwithstanding the disparity of their ages; Harry being only twenty-one, Phillips thirty. In comradeship such as this, age goes for very little, and it is doubtful if the thought of the considerable difference occurred to either, except as a passing topic in conversation. There were other differences: before the War, Harry had never done any manual work, his friend had done nothing else (though some of it was highly skilled); the younger man's philosophy tended to idealism, the older man's to materialism; and while the former swore little, blasphemed not at all, and rarely employed obscenities as oaths, the latter used language so startling, so biting, so realistic that whenever he began cursing, all within ear-shot ceased from talking in order to listen to this wonderful, horrible flow of words, as rapidly varied as it was uniformly picturesque, with English, American, Spanish and Australian terms intermingled. Phillips never let his anger or his indignation smoulder : he vented it immediately with a volcanic luridness and power until he and it were exhausted. These foul, scorching, sardonically humorous outbursts were as a safety-valve, and if there be a God, he will surely forgive Felipé readily, for he was brave, honest and honourable, kind and considerate, sympathetic, self-sacrificing ; he was courteous to women and he honoured his parents ; and after long, exceptionally continuous and arduous service, he died in battle exactly ten weeks before the Armistice. Brusque and often violent in manner, he had a warm and tender heart : apparently so tough in composition, he was in reality highly-strung and sensitive, and he suffered mental agony in his gallant victory over fear. Of a middle height, he was big-boned, broad-shouldered, neither thin nor fat, and of a good carriage ; very strong, quick, and active, withal deliberate in his movements ; dark hair, slightly sallow face, an unexaggerated moustache, flashing eyes, firm and well-chiselled features. In repose, his face was that of one of those strong silent heroes with whom the women novelists, perhaps in the wake of Seton Merriman or even of Byron and Charlotte Brontë, have made us so familiar ; but then he was not silent and he would probably have hurled some graphic epithet at the man who was so ill-advised as to call him a hero. In any other circumstance it showed a swift and supple play of features, as his eyes sparkled, shone or darkened; yet he rarely gesticulated and never gestured. If he were excited, his voice was loud, clear, commanding, constantly vibrating; at times it had a resonantly metallic note, but never did it become strident or displeasing: in ordinary conversation, it was low, rich, attractive, hinting of energy held in control. Little wonder, then, that Harry delighted in the talk of his friend, who combined emotion, delicate fancy and searching imagination with an unusually wide and profound experience of men and women, places, things, and with a daring powerful realism; one who wielded the rapier and the club with equal dexterity: one who, glancing from earth to heaven, ranged from a spontaneous summary of a play or criticism of an opera, to a curt reference to a ribald incident in Japan or a *fait divers* in Paris, from an enthusiastic account of a country retreat in California to the description of a scene on the South African veldt, or from a luminous insight into the mystery of life and death to a scathing denunciation of some military stupidity.

The disembarkation was timed for 11 p.m. It was a warm evening in mid-September, with no light save that of the stars. Fuller information might have been given to the men, who did not know what to expect. Ignorance in these matters may possibly be bliss but it is certainly folly. If trouble were expected, why not say so? If there were no danger, why not reassure inexperienced troops, who in point of fact inclined to believe that thrilling events were to ensue soon after they landed? If the Turks had known where and when a disembarkation was being made, they could have rendered the operation difficult and perilous : they didn't, and there was not the slightest reason to suppose that they did. Lighters conveyed the men ashore. They assembled, waited a long while, and, led by a guide, Harry's company marched by way of the beach to the position that they were to occupy for about a month. Ignorant as to their distance from the enemy, but aware that no danger threatened, they sank down and fell asleep ; the day had been a full one, they had not slept for at least twenty hours; the excitement, though restrained and chiefly of the imagination, had been considerable : and there is little that fatigues more quickly and insidiously than excitement.

When they awoke they found themselves in a sloping valley, perhaps forty yards across and seventy long with a ridge about a hundred feet high on three sides of them, the ascent being moderately steep ; the bottom was covered with grass, the sides with bushes and a few stumpy trees. The mouth of this depression lay five hundred yards from the sea, whereas, at the landing point, the hills were almost mountains with their base eighty yards or less from the water. Here, then, they were to camp, resting most of the day and making a useful sunken road from dusk, or soon after, until two or three in the morning. An agreeable life, with little of danger. It is true that " Johnny Turk " sent over a few light shells once or twice and killed a man, and that if one went in the day-time for water one was liable to be peppered with shrapnel ; but the enemy had about the same amount of ammunition as we had, and that was precious little : he reserved his bigger guns for the cruisers and the monitors (the latter—somebody called them "impudence afloat"—came in very close to the shore) that trained their guns on his trenches. Harry was one of those who ran the gauntlet for water; being ignorant of the deadly nature of shrapnel, he thought it rather a joke that his bucket was pierced in two places on the way to the well, yet he sufficiently appreciated the situation to take refuge awhile under a bank near the well. The shells that fell into the depression dropped on the nearest slope and the farther side, so scaring the battalion doctor that he removed to the opposite side and had a place excavated and built up with sand-bags: he was prudent, but prudence at that stage closely resembled cowardice. Moreover, one shell dropped just at the side of the entrance to the shelter occupied by Harry and Phillips; a very small shell; presumably from a kind of mountain-battery. Phillips was dozing inside when it burst. "I was a little scared," he told Harry, "but we'll stay right here, for it's highly improbable that we'll get another so close." The shelter consisted of a hollow nine feet long, three feet wide at the entrance and five at the back, and four feet high. It was covered with earth laid over close-set branches and several ground-sheets; the latter had been discovered by Phillips on the shore. A little job like this was a joy to such an ingenious handy fellow. The two friends made themselves as comfortable as anyone under the rank of an officer. On the earthen floor they had placed their own ground-sheets, and over these, Harry's blanket, while when they slept they used Felipé's as a cover; if the air were chill, a greatcoat provided additional warmth. Back in the small hours, from road-building, they

" turned in " and slept till perhaps eight o'clock : this was not sufficient rest to keep them going ; therefore, like the others, they usually dozed awhile in the early afternoon. Breakfast about eight-thirty, dinner about four hours later, tea about six o'clock. In the mornings, odd jobs, such as light fatigues, cleaning of equipment. The weather was excellent, with an occasional heavy shower ; the heat considerable, the flies numerous and unhealthy ; diarrhœa was common, enteric and typhoid only too frequent. Harry, as was inevitable, soon learnt the discomfort that can be caused by vermin. He did not at first realise the meaning of the strange tickling and itching, but he was soon enlightened. After a while, disgust became displeasure, and displeasure faded into the bored acceptance of an unavoidable drawback ; nevertheless, he always kept his distaste for the necessary process of " chatting." The food was inferior, with a nimiety of rice. Fortunately the water was fairly good : the units encamped on the shore drew it from the wells, which, however, were wholly unequal to the needs of those in the trenches on the hills ; for the latter, much of the supply came principally from Egypt, since even the water-station established around a newly-sunk artesian well was inadequate.

Gallipoli in the summer may be described as subtropical, with a heat neither ideal nor intolerable : in the autumn it is in some ways a most attractive place : in the winter there are heavy rains, frequent snow, and a low temperature. The Evacuation of Gallipoli was not merely a triumph of strategy, a retreat from an equivocal and unprofitable situation ; it was almost a necessity, for the losses during the winter would have been extremely heavy owing to illness and frost-bite, while it is probable that fresh meat would often have been wanting, the general supply of provisions uncertain; possibly those flimsy landing-stages would have been swept away in the frequent storms (it is a nasty coast for some three months), and one hardly likes to think what would have happened to the paths, in places little better than bridle-tracks, leading from the shore up those precipitous slopes. It is difficult to imagine the plight of the men if, in the worst of the winter, such mines had been fired as that which destroyed some three hundred Australians late in November, for the British force had little but an exposed and narrow shore behind them. It seems to be the fashion in these days to belittle Kitchener, but when, after spending a few hours on Gallipoli, he decided on the evacuation, he proved once more his extraordinary power of visualising a situation and his commendable ability to come to a rapid decision.

Apart from sickness, then, life in this little-known part was pleasant until about the end of October, when the weather began to deteriorate. Harry and Felipé made the most of it, and were particularly happy for the fortnight or so during which the men were allowed to cook their own meals. Strange how much further the proper army-ration goes if one handles it oneself than if the cooks have the disposal thereof, and this implication applies hardly less to the fighting areas than to base-camps, despite the fact that food cannot very well be sold in the former circumstances: even when we can be certain that there is absolutely no malversation of provisions, army cooks are as a rule wasteful. It was a blessing when one passed from such uneconomical, clumsy cooking to that of the company-cookers. Felipé, a rare hand at an extemporised meal, taught Harry how to deal with such simple food as theirs. After lunch, they smoked and talked awhile. Everything under the sun came up for discussion, and their experiences, past and present (this, of course, was where Felipé shone), added variety to the already various conversational fare. Very few books were to be had, but such as were in the company found their way sooner or later to *Notre Repos* (as the Onslow-Phillips habitation was called). Occasionally, they were put on light fatigues throughout the day, a variation that appealed to them, for once tea had been eaten—if prepared by themselves, enjoyed ; if dished up by those incompetent, bungling cooks, endured—they had the evening to themselves. They would saunter about for a time, perhaps down by the shore ; on returning they might sit outside their "possie," yarning or enjoying the evening breeze ; then, having made themselves ready for the night, they would converse and argue, smoke and be silent. Sometimes when the food had been exceptionally bad or scanty, they delighted in drawing up menus for a thoroughly alluring "Barmecide banquet." This phrase recalled Dickens to mind, for did he not use it once or twice ? To give an added piquancy to the pictured meal, they would attempt to compose a menu solely of Dickensian dishes : they found the roast turkey and beef, the beer and cheese peculiarly adapted to the countering of malnutrition. One night they sketched a Shakespearean menu. On waking next morning, Filipé exclaimed : "Damn that meal at Stratford-on-Avon! It has given me a liver." After that, they confined themselves to the nineteenth century or to the unaided efforts of their imagination. Nor were these meals debauches. They detailed and arranged the table-furniture artistically and tasted the dishes rather as *gourmets* than as *gourmands*, the wines as connoisseurs and not as drunkards. "My sherry has the most exquisite bouquet," said Harry; "mine," reparteed Filipé, "smells like nothing on earth; a very inferior vintage. John," he cried to a non-existent butler, "take this away and get me a bottle from the bin at the back." Imaginary conversations, less formal, less consecutive, less impressive, less stylised, and presumably less witty than those of the Landor brothers, were improvised by these two over the coffee and liqueur that never were on sea or land. The two best, in their opinion, were one between a successful lawyer (Harry) and a great explorer (Felipé) and a particularly heated debate between an eminent scholar (Harry) and a rich *viveur* (Filipé). After the chartreuse, they linked arms and joined the ladies: the older man imitated a match-making dowager, a countess dabbling in social work, a young hostess managing her first *soirée*, a débutante on the eve of her presentation. He was inimitable in these satires, parodies and pastiches. Yet Harry contributed convincing reproductions of the talk of church-workers, the affected curate, blue stockings, the shy maiden, the woman who talks unceasingly to hide her emptiness, and the sentimental old maid. The general conversations between the ill-matched members of an accidental group were occasionally attempted, but it is difficult to keep alive this sort of desultory chatter with its ineptitudes, its unappreciated epigrams, its "dropping of bricks," and its cynical gossip. Felipé had the wider range. He often sent his companion into roars of laughter with his "conversations on the telephone," in which he was enviably versatile. His best numbers in this kind were the making of assignations, the hasty invitation to dinner to fill a gap, the fuddled attempts of a young fop, after a late and heavy night, to learn from a fellow convivialist exactly what he had done or left undone the previous evening, the crude endeavours of a country bumpkin to make love to a cross telephone-operator. If one could have memorised or taken down Felipé's brilliant talk and "turns," one's fortune would certainly be made; but such a thought never occurred to Harry. His own share was too large to permit him to become a "Gallipoli-Boswell," and he enjoyed it all too keenly to have wished to do any such thing. When now he recalls those days and nights, he likes to think that what is perhaps the world's loss is certainly his own gain.

At times it was hunger, not for decent food, but for feminine company. They talked of woman and of women. They discussed and argued. "They are the very devil," said Felipé, "but necessary—and charming." Harry's knowledge of women was slight, his friend's comprehensive. Felipé related many of his experiences but never mentioned names: he would have been the last man in the world to boast of his success with women and he never spoke of them personally if he were in a group: he might, in a general discussion on their emancipation, exclaim: "Women are all right if kept in their proper place—in bed," or "Women always have been 'emancipated' in their sexual relations, but now they are beginning to talk about their so-called freedom." He appeared to have slept with a matron of the hospital that sheltered him in South Africa; to have lived for a week with the young and beautiful, cultured, exquisite, and wholly delightful mistress of an American multi-millionaire in a luxurious flat in New York ("Ah, Harry," he mused, "her breath was as sweet as her breasts, her embraces serpentine in the way she folded herself about me: love with her was full of perilous delights"); to have sampled the promiscuous favours of the geisha girls of Japan ("They make love, in the purely physical sense, better than any other women in the world . . . and with it all a flower-like grace"); to have excited the passion of Spanish beauties in the Argentine ("But one had to mind one's step"); to have lingered a week in the Blue Mountains of Australia in the company of a society-woman from Sydney ("She had the fascination and the aptitude for love of all the heroines of Elinor Glyn and Victoria Cross rolled into one"); to have had his first "affair" at the age of fifteen. Yet if he were a masterful sensualist, he was neither rake nor profligate ("I have never seduced an innocent girl"); never a slave to his passions, he so dominated them that he always had himself in hand. In the women that he loved, mere physical charm was not enough: "A woman without a heart or a mind will perhaps serve for the lust of an evening, but to survive the reaction she must be able to interest a man in other ways, to hold him without appeal to his animal self." Felipé had never been either married or engaged, and Harry suspected that he treated his loves of a week or a month with much of the tenderness and chivalry and true companionship that he would have observed towards a wife.

Towards the end of October, the company joined the rest of the battalion in the trenches; the ascent of those rugged hills offered much to interest them. They soon settled down to the new life. Trench warfare on Gallipoli was, normally, a mild affair, compared with that of the second half of the war in France and Belgium. Bombs were few: had they been numerous, the story would have been different, for the trenches ranged from only twenty-five to about a hundred yards apart. In some of the underground galleries, a sentry never knew just when one of the enemy might come upon him at the end of a comparatively straight stretch of ten or fifteen yards, or, if he were posted at a bend, he had to be constantly on the watch lest a Turk should come round the corner. Mining and counter-mining in so restricted an area meant that one always had to guard against sudden encounters. It was only a day after moving into the trenches that one of the miners provided Harry with his first sight of a man killed and mutilated in war, the victim of a bomb. He was a powerful fellow, easily the strongest in his platoon, full of life, violent in word and deed, a declared atheist, a loyal comrade and one of the bravest men in the company. Part of his head was caved-in and he had a ghastly wound in the breast. To see him lying there on a stretcher, still and horrible on a lovely autumn afternoon, gave Harry a shock. He gazed for a moment in pity, shuddered, and passed on. There was no time for morbid reflection. But he never forgot that scene, and he resented the pious remark of some rigid Methodist: "God cut him off in his pride because of his blasphemies." If, therefore, there was (apart from the landing, the charges, and sickness) no great loss of life on Gallipoli, there certainly was a good deal of excitement. The nights were not wholly peaceful, the worst for Harry's battalion being that on which it had fifteen casualties: "Johnny Turk" must have been making bombs—in structure they mostly corresponded with the jam-tin bombs employed by the Australians—for some days. During the hour before the dawn, every available man stood-to, a duty all the more imperative in that an unexpected, well-concealed and fiercely sustained rush might easily have carried all before it and swept the British troops from off that narrow plateau and down those precipitous slopes. Like his companions, Harry found the Turk a clean and chivalrous fighter.

He and Felipé scouted round for a dug-out and had the luck to discover a large one, built, of course, by the unit that had previously occupied this part of the line, but missed by the officers of their own company, the entrance being long, dark, narrow and rather low. "You can never tell a dug-out by its door-way," thought Harry. Having gained the inside, they found that they could stand erect. The dug-out itself was roomy, about ten feet long by nine wide; there was actually a sky-light of fine wire-netting, a foot square, let into the middle of the roof, which was of virgin earth and sufficiently thick to hold together but by no means thick enough to resist the impact of a shell. Two natural couches of clay flanked the greater part of each side, while a third linked them up at the far end ; in other words, a ledge two feet from the ground and thirty inches wide skirted the greater part of the walls of which it formed a portion. It is true that the rain and snow came in at the skylight, that the walls were damp, and that they had no brazier, but, comparatively, it was palatial. The two friends were acutely aware that they could not hope to keep this dug-out for themselves unless they had a third : they decided to invite a most likable young corporal of their acquaintance. A wise move in two senses, for he turned out to be an even finer and more attractive fellow that they had imagined, and, as he knew one of the officers, he managed to ward off several designing " one pip " lieutenants. It was not often that all three were there at one time, for more than a few minutes, since their duties rarely coincided ; the dinner-hour brought them together more than anything else. Harry and Felipé, however, were frequently off duty at the same period, and they renewed their old intimacy. The corporal was in no way " odd man out," but, orthodox in religion and provincial in morals, he did not welcome the free discussion of theological and philosophical problems, the daring speculation and talk about women into which the others often dropped, yet to be fair to him (and it was very easy to be that) he was neither sectarian nor prude. He simply lacked the broad-mindedness of his mates.

At the end of November, Harry went down to a bad attack of jaundice. Felipé brought him his meals and looked after him so quietly, so effectively and so gently that once or twice he turned his face to the wall lest his friend should see the tears in his eyes.

"With a love passing that of women" is a phrase that, applied to affection between men, bears for the sophisticated an equivocal meaning: so let us understand that the natural, rich, profound, sympathetic affection between Harry and Felipé was beautiful in its completeness, its durability, its joyous companionship, its readiness for mutual service. Neither, at any time during their three years' friendship, spoke to the other of his regard. There was no need. After their separations, for illness and wounds intervened, they sought each other immediately, ate and slept and yarned together as of yore. Well, Harry became so ill that at last he had to drag himself to the medical officer, who immediately sent him to a field hospital; a day later—it was the 2nd of December—he left the Peninsula, for he had also developed para-typhoid. On the hospital-ship he was confined to his bunk, and in the auxiliary hospital in Heliopolis he was, for a fortnight, a very ill man. Then a cist in his neck, into which the cold had penetrated just before he left Gallipoli, led to ear trouble, and he had to be transferred to the principal hospital, the Grand Palace Hotel. A magnificent building with spacious halls, lofty roofs, glistening chandeliers, delicate carving, and marble stair-cases. He was there a fortnight, in bed all the time, for he was still much debilitated. He read so much that the Sister scolded him. Mainly French books, for he managed to persuade a visitor to bring him some volumes from the *Collection Nelson Française*. Most of all he enjoyed de Vogüé's *Jean d'Agrève*: its exquisite, flowing style, its beautiful phrasing, its gripping, passionate and tragic story delighted him. It made such an impression on him that, before the war was over, he had read the same author's *Maître de la mer*, *Les Morts qui parlent*, and the collection of Russian stories in the same series.

Thence, Harry was sent to the big convalescent hospital at Helouan, where he remained a fortnight. A rather uncomfortable place, with small grounds, very little for the men to do, and few books to read ; when once or twice a mist-like shower fell, they were nonplussed. The food was very good. He was not sorry when he left for the convalescent camp at Ghezireh ; this was about the third week of January, 1916. After perhaps a fortnight, during which he took part in the short marches and parades, he was put on mess-orderly work for a month : he was still far from strong ; this job could not be described as fatiguing. He had plenty of time to himself and once or twice a week he trammed into Cairo on leave. He either strolled about and had a meal there or betook himself to one of the two passable cinemas ; on one occasion he had the good luck to see Flaubert's *Salammbo* filmed. Two Sunday mornings he went to a " Concert Symphonique," the orchestra of thirty-five being excellent. In March the camp was moved to Tel-el-Kebir, where he remained a week or two before he sailed for France, some time after the general exodus thither. It was a very small transport, with all the men sleeping in bunks. The food was extremely poor. Harry and his three cabin-mates (decent fellows all) reviewed the situation and decided that if they could " get round " a steward to bring them food from the officers' mess for a sum not too extortionate, they would have all their meals in the cabin. The " fly " one of the four, a short, perky, city-bred man, captured a steward and settled the affair: the steward was to receive one pound for the voyage from Alexandria to Marseilles; he took the risk and paid nothing for the food, which, it may be added, was worth much more than one pound. Those four enjoyed the trip, what with the perfunctory parades, the absence of fatigues, and the liberal supply of tobacco and cigarettes that they had wisely purchased for the occasion. Harry had two good novels with him, but he spent much of his time listening to the yarns and reminiscences of his mates. The sea was calm, the nights lit by a moon near the full. The ship entered the harbour at Marseilles on a perfect night that set him a-dreaming of other things than war. About ten days were passed in quarantine at the foot of a low hill on the outskirts of the city. Route-marches, a little drill, and two bathes in the sea. On the last evening, most of the men broke camp and went into Marseilles. Harry with several friends walked idly along the main street, entered a cinema, had supper afterwards and reached the camp safely (by climbing a wall) at one o'clock in the morning.

The journey by train to Etaples was slow but amusing, for to travel for the first time through a country so rich in historical associations as France must interest even a lot of tired and uncomfortable soldiers. As Harry was one of the few that could speak French at all, although his French was pretty rotten when it came to speaking it, he found himself in demand for the purchase of bread, cakes, fruit and chocolates. The food provided on the journey was quite inadequate, nor was it much better at Etaples, where the troops went through courses of bayonet-fighting, route-marching, bombing, shooting, and several fancy exercises for which one never had any practical use. One was occasionally allowed into Etaples, a most unexciting township: Paris-Plage was reserved for officers. Three weeks of this were enough for Harry, and he left without regret for the front. Another disagreeable journey, but one took that for granted. From the rail-head, at which they arrived at dusk on a fair day in June, they were marched, almost without a halt, to their respective trenches, not far from Neuve-Eglise; all peered curiously at the shattered buildings of a hamlet two miles from the front trench. The walk through the communication trench was thrilling, but, as at the disembarkation in Anzac Cove, nothing happened. Since the night was tranquil, Harry slept through what little of it remained. Before he was definitely allotted his duties, he walked about getting his bearings for some distance on either side of his dug-out. He received a pleasing welcome from his mates, some of whom had been promoted even unto the rank of officers; several were no more; the corporal friend of Gallipoli days had been badly smashed-up and sent to England with a certain "ticket" for Australia. Phillips he soon ran to earth: they met quietly yet with a great gladness. Felipé was now the corporal in charge of the company's machine-gun section. "What made you join the machine-gunners, old man?"

"Well, you know that I spent three years in the American Navy as a twelve-inch gunner. Thought I'd like to handle something more heavy than a rifle. Then . . . all my expert knowledge, you wouldn't have me sinfully waste it?"

"Get along with you, you old humbug!"

II

THE SOMME

EVERY day they saw each other as opportunity offered. A full account of their experiences in the past six months was given. Felipé complained of the numerous wet days and ascribed the humidity to the piercing of low clouds by the numerous church-spires. Harry was sorry to have missed seeing the raid effected by his battalion. Some fifty chosen men trained for several weeks before they crept across No Man's Land (a matter of two hundred yards at this point) all "made up" as Australian aborigines in war-dress and carrying nothing but tomahawks, clubs and bombs —rifles were discarded as too clumsy. The exploit proved completely successful. The party reached the enemy trench without the alarm being given. With a hair-raising yell they leapt down, the bombers going to the entrances of the dug-outs, the others flinging themselves on the soldiers manning the trench. The Germans, horribly scared, were allowed no time to collect themselves: it is doubtful if any of them had ever seen an Aborigine, certain that none had seen one in the garb of war. In three minutes the trench was cleared, the bombs were cast into the dug-outs, while such of the occupants as survived and came to the entrance were tomahawked or clubbed on the head; at either end of the section attacked, there stood an expert bomber with a liberal supply to keep the coast clear; then, at a word from an officer in charge, they snaked their way back to their own line with a speed that was the result of long and strenuous practice. Not one of the party was killed, only three were wounded—

slightly at that. If the Scottish soldiers were known among the Germans as "the Mad Women from Hell," what must have been the impression caused by this raid! It was reported at German Headquarters that the foray had been made by genuine Aborigines led by a white officer, an error that, soon rectified amongst the staff, caused a wild canard to circulate among the "Fritz" troops. Such rumours were no less frequent among the conflicting armies than among the civil populations. Often they were begun by spies and disaffected persons, often they arose from a mistake or a misunderstanding, and now and again some wag started one. Harry collected all the "pferfies" (as they were known to the Australians) he could, studied them, and made up several perfectly ridiculous and innocuous ones, which he set going himself: they usually came back to him grossly exaggerated or changed almost beyond recognition. He regarded this attempt not merely as a joke but as an intriguing, amusing, and enlightening experiment upon the credulity of the human race: it is much more credulous during a war than in time of peace; in days of stress, the more picturesque (therefore the more unlikely) a rumour is, the more easily does it gain attention and credence.

In this sector near Armentières, the line was usually quiet. Every few nights, however, "Fritz" got busy with his mine-throwers, the "Minnies" of the soldiers' vocabulary. Nasty things. Luckily they possessed only a limited accuracy of aim. Occasionally, if the movement in the Australian trenches were too blatantly obvious to be tolerated, a battery of German seventy-sevens discharged a few rounds, but generally these "whizz-bangs" (there is no more happily invented term in military slang than this) did no damage. Harry enjoyed the pastoral calm of the summer landscape as he looked through his periscope; for hours in the day-time the silence would be unbroken save for the snipers' shots at long intervals. For all the apparent somnolence, no man poked his head over the top with impunity, the snipers in either trench being deadly in the rapidity and the precision of their aim. Some of the "out-West" Australians were marksmen of repute, and the best of them drifted into the company, battalion, or brigade snipers: they were no less at home with the slow, deliberate shot directed with a telescopic sight than with the sudden "pot shot." These two extremes were reconciled where a rifle was so fixed that its bullets necessarily hit a certain point in the opposite line; immediately a man's head appeared at this dangerous corner or that dip in the parapet, the sniper pressed the trigger. But it doesn't do for a fixed rifle to remain long in one place, for the enemy invariably spots it or infers it sooner or later. The post then receives an unrequested visit from a "whizz-bang." Exit sniper.

Near the middle of July, the whole division was ordered South. The battalions travelled by different roads. They marched the whole way, by a not too circuitous route, to the Somme; the first night was spent at Bailleul, one of the liveliest of towns. After three days by way of Merville and Wavrans, they were allowed—it was a Sunday—to halt and rest in the simple hamlet of Beaudricourt. On they went for three days, the night's break coming at Authieule and Warloy-Baillon. They remained four days at

Vaux-sur-Somme, then a semi-deserted village, close to the Somme itself, in which, one very hot day, the company bathed at a point three miles downstream. Harry had seen a good deal of Felipé on the march, and they spent as much of those four days together as possible. Once as they were strolling through the village, they passed company headquarters, outside of which stood, rather tipsy, one of the officers. Harry, the closer, saluted; Felipé, either because he failed to notice or because it was one of his moody days, did not salute. The officer called indignantly after them: "Stop, there! Corporal Phillips, how dare you pass without saluting? Do it now." Whereupon, without a word, Felipé performed, with an exaggerated precision and gusto, the American cavalry salute, so different in its ornateness from the ordinary English. The officer was furious. "Corporal Phillips, you will consider yourself confined to quarters for twenty-four hours. Private Onslow, I charge you to conduct the corporal there." Felipé, standing a moment with a dangerous gleam in his eyes, walked off immediately. Harry took his arm affectionately and murmured: "Come along, old man! Don't mind that drunken beast." They strode off. It occurred to them that the officer was so fuddled that he would forget what he had said. They therefore continued their stroll without entering the "place of durance vile"; they did not, however, believe in tempting providence by passing headquarters again that day. The incident reminded Harry of what his pal had told him on his return to the battalion. One day in early May, up on the Armentières sector, Felipé was sitting in the sun employed in making some ingenious model. An English staff-officer happened along. " What are you doing there ? "

" As you see, I'm constructing a model."

" Do you think it's of any use ? "

" Not the slightest, sir."

" Then why do you waste your time thus ? "

" Because it amuses me," very curtly.

" But can't you find other amusements ? "

" I don't see the obligation, sir. And what is more, I would rather do something like this than talk shop or sit in a group telling smutty stories, beyond which and reading (you may know how extensive our library is) one has practically nothing to do in one's leisure."

The officer, taken aback, turned without a word and continued his inspection. This product of one of the major public schools and Sandhurst, who belonged to the rapidly decreasing *haw-haw* type, was not accustomed to being addressed as though the speaker might easily be his equal mentally and morally. A somewhat similar incident was to occur in the spring of 1917 : Harry and Felipé were moving from the front line to an assembly-point about four miles behind ; " Fritz " had been very active, many the casualties, so judge the look on Felipé's face when the battalion medical officer (who had never been seen in the front trench) smugly expressed his hope that all was well with " the boys," and imagine the trenchant, searing phrases of Felipé's reply! The doctor visibly withered, gasped, and then, mumbling something propitiatory in his walrus-moustache, resumed his way, so staggered that he apparently did not think of placing this volcanic corporal under arrest. It is, moreover, an invidious action to arrest a soldier of known integrity, well-tried gallantry, and considerable usefulness, especially when he is so terribly in the right.

Those four sun-drenched days in the village on the Somme were the last easeful, happy days for many in the battalion. Arcady was left behind: the narrow shady streets, the old barns, the slope from the village, the flat lands covered with grass and crops. One fair day's march brought them to their bivouac some four miles behind the line, where they remained three days, resting, doing fatigues, preparing for the attack which they were to make along with two other battalions of their brigade. On the last day, their packs (the common Australian name for the knapsacks) were taken to Albert, there to be stored until the battalion should leave the front for a spell.

At eight o'clock on a warm, clear evening, late in July, 1916, the battalion set off for the front line. They moved up with a short interval between platoons, two hundred yards or so between companies. Before long they came to the entrance of Sausage Gully, where, since the First Australian Division's successes of a week earlier, a large number of cannon had been massed. An artillery duel rendered every night "a potential starting-point for heaven or hell," but no special activity was to precede the attack; guns were to play on the enemy trenches for a few minutes. The bright idea of a senior officer anxious to win distinction. Despite the brigade-major's declaration that it was murder on a large scale, the other carried the day (the detail leaked out shortly afterwards); yet he retained his command. The men, however, had no precise idea as to what faced them; and that was well. The approach to the jumping-off point increased in difficulty. After the broad track of Sausage Gully and those reassuring rows of guns, at first the six-inch, the beautiful sixty-pounders, and, at the extremity of the Gully, the least advanced of the eighteen-pounders—with the artillerymen symbolic in the growing obscurity—they passed into a communication-trench, which, for some distance high, comfortably wide, and in general well-made, finally became rough and arduous. In places the trench was much too low, one kept tripping over pieces of wire or fallen clumps of earth. Here a parapet (if the unsandbagged forward side could be rightly termed a parapet) was partly blown away, there a parados was reduced to a low mass of powdered soil. A few men of another brigade were stationed in tiny cavities at the base of the trench : they watched with taciturn interest the passage of these fresher troops. The going became difficult ; in places the ground sagged, and after several of these sinkings one realised that men lay smothered beneath the tramping feet. The roar of guns grew louder, Very lights and others appeared close at hand. The last half mile was along what served as the front line, for it could not be called a trench, since it was so low that it resembled a dry, unimportant and neglected ditch. The trees stood out like giant skeletons in the flashes of light : the men were in a small wood, the leaves withering, the trunks and branches torn by shells. Shells now began to fall on either side—or most of them did. Just before they reached the point at which they were to halt, Harry's section passed a tragic group of four non-commissioned officers : one killed, two very severely wounded, one temporarily dazed by a shell that had exploded several yards away. Good soldiers all. The men then left the front line and lay waiting about seventy yards in advance of it : that distance placed them barely yet satisfactorily out of reach of the shells that commenced to pour into the wood they had so providently quitted. At last, midnight came. The troops moved off across the large, level meadow towards the German trenches eight hundred yards away. For half the distance they were undiscovered, but then the outposts gave the alarm. These isolated men, sheltered in small pits, were soon overpowered ; Harry put a bullet into one, but suspected that, already dead, he stood propped against the side because he could not fall. Not until the enemy in his trenches was sure that the assailants were between him and his outposts did he dare to open fire with his machine-guns, for he had no wish to kill his own men. The Australians swept over the last three hundred yards, many dropping on the way ; but when they reached the trenches they found the barbed-wire entanglements almost intact. They sought the openings, and, in scattered groups and much diminished numbers, rushed on the trench. Nearly all perished. Among them was the captain of Harry's company : through a gap he led a party straight at the line of flashes from rifle and machine gun ; with his revolver he shot several Germans ; and he was slain on the very parapet as he waved on his men. A few managed to escape. But many—perhaps a quarter of the three battalions engaged—had stopped at a sunken road, which they proposed to defend. At a particularly dangerous bend, raked by machine-guns, they built several sandbag walls ; at almost every moment, someone pitched forward with a bullet through his brain. Among these defenders was Harry, who, contrary to orders, had stopped to ask a wounded man if he could do anything for him : he had been pierced through the stomach by a bullet. One of those army orders which doubtless had sufficient justification (for obviously it wouldn't do if everyone were to halt to aid a friend) but which revolted him, was that which said : "In an attack, nobody must stop to assist the wounded, however grave their need ; the stretcher-bearers will follow after an interval and attend to the casualties." Well, after frantic efforts to make themselves safe, the troops were recalled. Many of these survivors fell before they regained the deeper communication trench, for not only were No Man's Land and the sunken road by which a number retreated swept with a deadly machine-gun fire, but the front-line, a pitiful makeshift at this point, was bombarded with seventy-sevens and five-nines. Either no definite order was given as to where the men were to assemble or else it reached but a few ; yet as they could go out by only one path, or rather in only one direction, there was no danger of their being dangerously scattered. Harry, with several others, found a large group of the survivors gathering by the roadside ; there they waited for an hour to allow the stragglers to come up. They were joined by a small fatigue-party from their own company, men who had cursed because they were debarred from taking part in the attack ; among these was Felipé, who, on seeing Harry, grasped him silently by the hand and then, after gazing a moment, exclaimed : "My God, man, you look as if you had been through hell!"

"Not as bad as that, Felipé, but damned near it!"

Only five hundred were left unkilled and unwounded out of the two thousand five hundred assailants. The remnant of Harry's battalion reached the bivouac between nine and ten o'clock. A messenger had been sent on ahead, so that, soon after they arrived, a hot and generous meal was served. Harry looked at his fellows and was startled to see how haggard they were, how drawn their faces. Breakfast over, they fell fast asleep and were allowed to rest until six o'clock, when tea—a more substantial one than usual—arrived. The Colonel addressed what remained of his battalion: about ninety had not participated in the assault; there were perhaps one hundred and sixty survivors from among those who had. No word of blame: both because blame would have been as rash as it was unjustifiable, and because he was genuinely moved. A week later he was himself severely wounded; having been absent from the first attack, he probably felt that it was up to him to lead his men into the second.

The day following the return from this disaster, equipment was examined, damaged parts replaced. Otherwise, the men were permitted to rest until the evening, when the battalion had to take up its share in digging trenches. During the next four days, on the first of which arrived a detachment of some two hundred and fifty men to reinforce the battalion, they worked at night building a new communication trench and a kind of reserve front-line over a length of almost a quarter of a mile. Presumably it was to receive the adjacent troops of the actual and continuous front line if "Jerry" (alias "Fritz") made it too hot for them. It was always advisable to finish these jobs in one night if possible, for the aviators usually spotted any new activity. Usually, also, it was impossible to finish such work in one short summer night. On the second of the evenings spent on each of these two undertakings, therefore, the men went up the line with the uneasy feeling that it might well be for the last time. When once they arrived (immensely relieved if they did not have to endure a barrage), they set to with a desperate energy and finished in two or three hours what in normal circumstances they would have regarded as a satisfactory full night's work; if, as generally happened, the strong finished their allotted portion before the weak, they assisted them gladly. On the former of these occasions, "Jerry" put over some "whizz-bangs" just as they were about to start off for the bivouac, killed two and wounded five. On the second, the more dangerous, they got away without having been peppered: five minutes later they heard a tidy little "strafe" going on behind them—the scene of their recent operations was being shelled with a few five-nines as well as with seventy-sevens. A sigh of relief like to a summer breeze issued from a hundred parched throats.

During this week of partial calm, the two friends were inseparable when their free time coincided. Once they walked to the nearest canteen and treated themselves to a "spread" of macaroons and preserved fruit, with Ideal Milk instead of cream. Except for several casual showers and one drizzly day the weather remained brilliantly fine. To drop to sleep at the dawn, in air as fresh and clear as that in an English field, was a joy to those weary with the night's labours. Harry's and Felipé's ground-sheets were erected in the form of an awning, and usually the rifleman returned from fatigue to find the machine-gunner asleep. " All right, old man ? " the corporal would murmur as Harry lay down beside him. Felipé had insisted on a full account of the attack that failed. " At any rate," he remarked, " we may be sure that the stunt now in preparation will be much better managed. Another massacre of one's own men would justify a mutiny : to hell with an officer who, for a paltry medal, will use his troops as gun-fodder and who, while they win the medal for him or get killed off, skulks in a deep dug-out over a glass of rum ! "

" Agreed ; but after all, there are very few of these fire-eaters at second hand. The great majority of the officers are thoroughly prepared to do their bit ; and you must confess that most of them do it well."

" That's only right : half a dozen like that skunk—the wholesale butcher !—would among them succeed in performing the delicate operation of converting battalions into platoons."

It is true that the brigade as a whole was never again to be so used ; but the greater part of a battalion, in the latter half of the 1916-1917 winter, was sent over in the mud and slush to capture a village on the Somme front, not far from the battle-ground of Pozières. In this case it was an incompetent and bungling officer who thirsted for blood ; he too remained in his dug-out : half of the men were bogged on the way across, to perish either from the broom-like fire of machine-guns or from the bitter cold ; those who reached the objective had to resort to the bayonet or to use their rifles as clubs since they were choked with mud; they despatched a few of the enemy but the majority of them were killed or captured; at the most, one in ten returned safely to the trench from which he had crawled with the aid of a ladder and with sore misgiving at his heart. The officer who was responsible for this decimation of his own men, for this most damnable holocaust exacted to appease mediocrity's hunger for fame, was court-martialled and shot? Your mistake. He was not even cashiered. Removed from the command of as gallant a set of soldiers as one could wish to lead, he was but relegated to a safe job elsewhere. "God save us from our officers!" had been the bitter cry of those who survived this mid-winter madness, and one almost fears to dwell on what must have been the thoughts of those who slowly froze to death in No Man's Land that night. The other disgraceful affair, that of July, 1916, was the origin of the cynical remark that one so often heard applied to absentees at informal roll-calls of the unlucky battalions involved (a saying that soon spread to other units): "Hanging on the barbed-wire."

The night of August 4th-5th was not to see Harry working near the front-line on a fatigue. His whole division, along with some English troops, was to deliver an attack on a front of approximately five miles; his battalion bearing in mind the position of a certain windmill was to jump off from slightly in front of the village of Pozières, which, by this time a mass of ruins, had itself constituted an area of successful carnage about a fortnight previously. These were in fact the two battles of Pozières, or rather they are known as such to the Australian units engaged therein.

Zero was fixed at 9.15 p.m., when the dusk had lost its kinship with day and was beginning to assume the character of night.

The men had been rested as much as possible ; a rapid yet thorough inspection of rifles and gear, distribution of extra cartridges (two belts apiece) and of Mills bombs (two, carried in the side-pockets, per man), and the delivery of general instructions occupied the hour immediately preceding the late dinner, served as close as possible to the final fall-in of the men in battle-order. There was no need to see if they carried the regulation amount of water, bully-beef and biscuits. The leadership of the companies and platoons differed greatly from that during the battalion's attack on the neighbouring sector so shortly before this second ordeal ; for instance, a new reinforcement officer that had led Harry's platoon with distinction and a rare courage, was now placed in charge of the company ; the senior corporal of the platoon was now its officer.

Just before the assembly at a quarter to three, Harry and Felipé shook hands. "The best of luck, old man!" Brief, final instructions were given, and at three sharp the battalion moved off on a hot and brilliant afternoon.

Just more than six circuitous miles at the most, and six hours in which to do them. Time was allowed for a halt about half-way and for a rest before the hop-over ; in military operations, a wide margin has to be left for unexpected delays, for changes of plan, and for the possibility of straying from the appointed track. As it happened, the allotted time was none too great. Since the battalion was one of those moved up just before the attack—you cannot have the front lines of a dangerous sector, liable to heavy shelling at any time, packed with men for more than a few hours—the march up to the jumping-off point was a ticklish business. Platoons were separated by considerable intervals; one didn't know just when a hostile aeroplane would spot the movement and cause a battery to open fire. Sausage Gully was crowded with guns, some well camouflaged, some naked to the gaze of heaven and of "Fritz": they were distinctly more numerous than before; several additional eighteen-pounder batteries were to be moved close up at the last moment, others were to come from far back to occupy the posts thus vacated; a sixty-pounder battery was settling into position as the battalion passed, and soon after they left the bivouac they had seen four six-inch naval guns being installed in a new emplacement; they had heard rumours of a battery of large-calibre howitzers situated a little to the rear of the bivouac. Everything pointed to an adequate artillery preparation and support: and as the enemy could not possibly have been blind to the increased activity behind the British line, it also meant that the opposition would be exceedingly warm. Yet Harry's company must have been less than half a mile from the front line before a battery began to caress them (Felipé's phrase) as the result of an aviator's reconnaissance. Several men were wounded and sent to the rear. The last two hundred yards of the communication-sap were unpleasant, for not only did it become little more than a hint for a trench but it offered several completely-exposed patches, one being across an iron-hard road. Just as they reached this point, "Fritz" began to make it very hot with "whizz-bangs" for the advancing party. Fortunately, just across and to the right of this road was a deep shelter-sap about fifty yards long: those who had already traversed or were in the act of traversing the road profited thereby, while the rest halted in the communication trench, which, as far as the crossing, was worthy of its name. After a twenty minutes' "strafing" from this battery and with a few casualties, the men resumed their approach. The remainder of the trench, subject to enfilade, took them a very short time to put behind them. On reaching the front line they walked some distance to the right and rested awhile, expecting that this was to be the jumping-off point. Then came a message to move to the left and to do so without delay: the men had felt that here was another error, for they were in an already well-occupied part of the line. Hurrying along the encumbered trench was difficult, curses punctuated their progress. As they drew near to the head of the communication-sap, shells began to fall around them, a few five-nines breaking the monotony of the "whizz-bangs"; they had to go a hundred yards past the junction before entering the newly-dug jumping-off sap, which ran out from the front line at an angle of some forty degrees. That short distance, however, was "warm going"; a number of men dropped to the ground, killed or badly wounded. At the very entrance into the new sap, Harry saw a sight that probably he will never forget: a shell had dislodged a heavy mass of earth on to the neck of a passing man; it had struck him with such force and felled him in such a manner that one side of his body remained wholly visible; the neck was horribly elongated. No wound; just the ghastly face with starting eyeballs, protruding tongue, the shoulders grotesquely distant from the jaws, and the neck so unexpectedly distended. After a fascinated glance, Harry pushed on, as indeed he had to do in order to avoid causing a hold-up in that infernal trench. Once they had passed the corner and were well in the sap, they felt comparatively safe: in fact "Jerry" did not shell it at all, unless perchance it were after the attack had commenced.

The men waited quietly. The distance across No Man's Land was about half a mile; they ought, at a steady double, to do it in six minutes. "Hold yourselves ready," ordered the major, whom Harry knew; they had not seen each other for some time, and when they met ten minutes earlier, they had exchanged a few words. On the tick of 9.15, when the dusk had gathered, a tremendous roar of guns was heard, the sound being preceded by the flash of the avalanche of shells falling on the German front line; some of the sixty-pounders and six-inch naval guns were searching the positions of the enemy's batteries. For four minutes this stream of shells from Sausage Gully poured into the first objective; the barrage was then lifted and put down on the second German line with a curtain fire of eighteen-pounders before and behind it, while the concentration on the known German batteries continued. But the foe had brought up many guns at the last moment, and he maintained a deadly discharge of shrapnel into No Man's Land, of ordinary shells into the British front lines and communication-trenches, of five-nines into the forward batteries, heavier guns on to the rearward. Meanwhile the troops swept on, beneath a rain of metal, towards the blaze of bursting shells; when the barrage was raised, they discovered the objective by the spits of flame from the few surviving riflemen and machine-gunners. After clearing the front-trench they proceeded, at scheduled time, to the second line, which they captured after a short struggle. They might also have captured some seventy-sevens if they had gone on a little further, but it was judged inadvisable to continue the advance.*

After clearing up the second line and repairing it against the attack which they knew would be made at dawn, the men obtained a few minutes' rest before the German guns opened fire and the field greys were seen advancing in that solid formation which the British avoided: not in a massed attack such as they launched in the early days of the War, but in a rashly close formation. Nevertheless, only half of them reached the Australians, who, after a dour hand-to-hand conflict, routed them. An hour later, another attack was made with the same result. For two days they held that severely-pounded trench. Their greatly-reduced numbers and their extreme fatigue rendered a relief necessary.

Felipé, who fought like a devil, was a tower of strength with that machine-gun section of his; at the end, he and one man remained to work the gun, but

* This is a practice which calls for military genius: the decision to attempt further progress may result in a notable success, but it may also lead to the advanced troops being surrounded: obviously, the smaller the gap that has been made in the enemy's line, the greater the danger that the assailants may be cut off: obviously, too, the deeper the penetration, the less chance there will be of retreating and the greater the exposure on either flank. Moreover, it requires a long time for the military machine to set in movement those units which flank the advancing troops.

Harry had been struck down not more than two hundred yards from the jumping-off sap. He kept close to his friend the major, who, seeing that the men were bunching together, shouted and waved instructions for them to deploy. Harry had run several yards to the right when he felt a blow as of a sledge-hammer on the extreme left side of his back. He dropped like a felled ox. Recovering from his momentary stupor, he reassured himself that, though there was a good deal of blood, the wound was not of the kind that makes one think of death. He saw his comrades moving as ghosts amid the smoke and as wizards amid the flashes of bursting shells ; they soon disappeared, yelling and shouting, from his view. He crawled to a shell-hole, for he did not in the least wish to become a receptacle for any more shrapnel pellets, or to stop the fragments of cases that were hurtling through the air. Feverish, he reached for his water-bottle. He found his hip wet with blood : the other blow was so severe that he simply hadn't felt this simultaneous wound. Nothing serious, evidently. "Must have that drink," he muttered invitingly. He lifted the bottle from its straps ; it seemed very light. Ah! now he saw what had happened. A second pellet had gone through it half-way down and into the fleshy part of his hip. He drank a little of the water, carefully replaced the bottle so that no more should escape. But heavy shells were dropping unpleasantly close ; he moved painfully some fifty yards nearer the middle of No Man's Land. That small distance made all the difference ; in a shell-hole he was safe from the machine-gun bullets. Snuggling into the broken ground, he listened awhile, noted that he could not yet regain the trench behind him, and dozed fitfully until the first hint of dawn. He perceived that the German fire on the front trench had ceased for the time being. Bent nearly double, for the wound in his back had grown stiff and sore, he walked slowly to the trench and along it. But just as he was about to leave by that hazardous communication-sap to an advance dressing-station, " Fritz " renewed his attentions : " More of his damned bouquets," grumbled Harry, as he took shelter, at this juncture, in a small dug-out holding already four wounded men. Five-nines. Some were falling into the wood around the communication-trench, others over an extent of perhaps a hundred yards of the old front line, the nearest dropping twenty to thirty yards away ; every fourth shell landed thus close, burst and shook the ground in a manner to exasperate the wounded men, who were impatient to have done with the din and the danger ; clods of earth fell at the entrance and on top of the dug-out, numerous jagged pieces of flying metal sang over their heads, several came whirring to within a foot of where they crouched. Once or twice during their enforced idleness, an inaccurate shell plonked into the ground only ten or twelve yards away and almost brought the shelter about their ears ; the explosion, which would have jarred a whole man severely but which was deadened a little by the walls of the dug-out, shook them painfully and made them grind their teeth. At last, the battery gave over. As soon as he had made sure of this, Harry set out through the torn trees, among the ruins of Pozières (not a wall remained standing), and along the further trench, having occasionally to step aside lest he should walk on a corpse ; he shuddered when he passed a private from his own battalion with half his head shot away, lying prone in the trench where, checked in his hasty advance, he had pitched forward. His wound dressed, he was put on a trolley and conveyed to a field-ambulance perched high among the trees on a rounded eminence. There he received something to eat and drink before proceeding by motor-ambulance to Warloy-Baillon, where, perhaps a fortnight earlier, his battalion had passed a night on their way to the front, and where Felipé and he had visited a deserted brewery. The stretchers were removed from the cars and laid on the ground; about the wounded (perhaps a score in this batch) thronged a detachment of soldiers; reinforcements who gazed, admiring and impressed, at these victims of the great battle of which they had heard vague rumours. "Hit in the back, severely wounded; looks bad," said one of them gravely as he stooped to look at Harry's ticket. Harry was dead-tired and desired only to rest. At this station the wounded were inoculated against tetanus, sorted out, and motored to the train that duly deposited them at Rouen.

There he remained for a week. One extracted the pellet lodged on the inner side of the thigh. "A near go," he reflected with a smile; "*idoneus nuper puellis* and all that sort of thing; embarrassment in answering solicitous enquiries as to the locality of the wound." He rejoined when he heard that it was "a Blighty one" as the Tommies used to say, "a Blighty" in the terser slang of his countrymen. Five days at the Cambridge Hospital at Aldershot. He was glad to leave that hot-bed of rules and regulations, where he had offended a sister. The morning inspection by the M.O. was due; she straightened and smoothed his bed; the wound in his back hurting him, he moved to ease the pain. In advance of the doctor (who, to judge by the respect shown him, might have been God Almighty) hurried the sister; seeing the state of Harry's bedclothes she scolded him wrathfully. "Sister, perhaps you would do better if you were to think less of the beds and more of your patients." The look she gave him indicated anger, surprise and recognition of the truth of his observation. He was transferred to a delightful V.A.D. hospital a few miles away: a large country-house standing in extensive grounds, meadow and lake and woodland. He stayed there five weeks and could have had longer. He wandered about the grounds, read, and lazed; visited the glorious Surrey uplands—the Devil's Punch Bowl, Godalming and the Hog's Back—one sunny afternoon early in September. How eagerly he surrendered to the charm of the English landscape, its quiet beauty, its surprising variety, its mellowness and its eternal youth; a rustic bridge over a small stream running like a silver thread between sunlit glades of secular tree and green-leaved bush; the ruins of an old abbey, vested with precious memories, fenced off from a meadow grazed by fat and sleepy kine; long straight lawns and long straight waters; hills covered with golden furze or autumn-tinted trees. Then a fortnight's leave; a visit to an old friend in Birmingham and a run through Warwickshire; the rest of the time in London, with many a theatre and a few good cafés. After that, a camp on Salisbury Plains, and the return to France.

III

THE BRIGADE OBSERVERS

Harry remained much longer at Etaples than he had expected. Measles brought a month in an isolation camp ; bad health caused him to be put on messenger and orderly-room work for two months ; someone else caught an infectious complaint which meant another three weeks in isolation. During this time he corresponded with Felipé. In fact it was not until March, 1917, that, the march from the rail-head being by way of Flers of bloody memory, he rejoined his battalion.

At first near Lagnicourt, he was for two months in and out of the trenches in front of Bullecourt, where the fighting could be pretty severe : ordinary trench-duty, laying a cable from just outside Noreuil, and so forth. To dig a trench for a cable, when it has to be taken right to the front line, is tantamount to risking an enfilade fire ; experiencing this on the second evening, as they were finishing the trench, they lost some good men. Much more acceptable was it to watch the heavy British shells bursting in Bullecourt and sending up diminutive clouds of dust and smoke.

Felipé was still his lovable self, more seasoned, more bitter and more volcanic when he broke out, but less frequent in his outbursts. He had been uninterruptedly in the thick of it since September, 1915, except for one leave. In the front trench, the two friends shared a " possie " ; in hutments they resumed the old ways. On one occasion, when the battalion was to be out for a fortnight, Harry, as the result of a " possible " in a shooting test, joined a school of instruction in sniping. After a few days, the brigade was recalled up the line, as things had gone wrong near Bullecourt. A night at Favreuil waiting for orders ; several fierce days in the line, and they were back again in hutments. A detachment of twenty men, with a corporal in charge, was sent to a rest-camp at St. Valéry-sur-Somme for the latter half of May : the corporal was Felipé, one of the men was Harry. Not a coincidence. An old pal of the latter's was adjutant ; he knew, of course, of their friendship —everyone in the battalion did ; he saw that Felipé badly needed a change of air and a rest, that Harry was none too fit ; hence their good fortune. The party, from near Mametz, walked across-country to the station at which they were to entrain ; they reached the town in the dusk, and the camp (two miles away) in the dark. A new camp ; tents to be pitched ; tea and stew ; finally a long, deep slumber. The fortnight was wholly delightful. In the morning " physical jerks," a short parade, or an hour's march ; the rest of the day free. Open camp was proclaimed, leave held automatically within a five miles' radius, and only the guard felt peeved. Felipé's party had twice to furnish a twenty-four hours' guard (once more than was fair) : as the corporal was unavoidably in charge, Harry asked to be included ; so once he did the orderly's work, which consisted in the very easy task of carrying food to the guard, and once he played at being sentry, for the sentry-go was rather a farce, since all that the men guarded was the orderly-room. During the first week, the inseparables visited St. Valéry-sur-Somme, famous as being the port from which William the Conqueror sailed to overcome Britain ; a small but pleasant old fishing town. They strolled about, saw most of what was to be seen, and sampled the pastry and the wine. In the second week, they bathed most mornings in the Somme; the weather being summery, the water was just sufficiently warm to make a dip enjoyable. On several afternoons they walked to neighbouring hamlets, to which hardly any of the others went. There they would march up to the door of a decent-looking cottage and enquire if they might have *petits pains* or *croissants* with butter, and *café au lait* or cider. "*Mais certainement, Messieurs*": after a shrewd glance. ("You see, Harry, we're obviously the genuine article, honest, God-fearing and polite . . . our charm of manner, too . . .") Upon which they were courteously seated at a table and within a few minutes served with a capacious bowl of coffee or a huge and brimming glass of cider, with the rest in proportion. If they felt too lazy for such excursions they would lie in the coppice flanking the camp and yarn, read and smoke. The sun filtering through the bright green leaves played about them, the warmth induced such a feeling of well-being as had not been theirs for many a long day, the scented air and May-blue sky brought a quiet joy to their hearts, the peacefulness and the absence of danger gave them a delicious sense of security, and the birds chirruping gaily applied yet another balm to their worn bodies and tortured nerves. Those golden hours would require the art of a Cunninghame Graham to do them justice; the tranquil felicity and the dear companionship come back to Harry with a dull pain when he thinks of Felipé, the closest, best-loved friend he ever had, lying in a cemetery in France. Those days were the last during which the two men were long and continuously together, for soon after their return to the battalion Harry was offered the choice of two jobs, the one or the other of which, owing to his general debilitation, he was bound to accept unless he desired to be so incapacitated that he would be sent to England as a "Class C." He was no hero, he suffered the torments of hell when in action, he only prevented himself on several occasions from becoming a deserter by pulling himself together by sheer force of will, but he wished to be of some use if he possibly could. The orderly-room clerk of his company, or a brigade observer. The former repelled, the latter attracted him. It is true that if he remained with the company he remained with his friend, but he felt that he could not sacrifice his self-esteem to his friendship: he talked the matter over with Felipé, who said: "You want to joint the Brigade Observers, don't you? I, too, think you should."

On the 31st of May, 1917, he was transferred to Brigade-Headquarters just as the division went out of the line for three months and a half; well had it deserved this respite. Brigade-Headquarters moved twice durıng this period, the first time to Bapaume, the second considerably further back. Each billet was in a pleasant district, and Felipé's battalion was never more than three miles away; they managed to see each other a couple of times a week, Harry usually making the journey since it was he who had the more leisure. The first of these billets was a hut, built in the grounds of a farmhouse attached to a small château in the village of Senlis, where they remained throughout June. Harry received his initiation in the art of observing, in which he proved an apt pupil, for not only had he fairly long service to his credit but he had always been watchful of military activities, subterfuges and methods ; the spade-work was familiar, the finer aspects he studied closely and with such success that by the end of February, 1918, his corporal declared him to be one of the three best observers in the section. In the long summer evenings he read or sauntered or watched the brigade boxing-tournaments. The second billet consisted of a tent high up on the hill that stands over the old ramparts at the side of the picturesque town of Bapaume, and their occupancy there was approximately co-terminous with the month of July. The healthiest, prettiest of all three stages. The observers' tent stood at the end of a short row pitched on a natural terrace overlooking the old moat, the walls of which were about sixty feet high. Overgrown with trees, bushes, ferns and long luxuriant grass, the sides were reminiscent of mediæval warfare only if one examined them closely ; no stream nor pool covered the bottom of the moat, where sometimes informal shooting-competitions were held or groups of men smoked and talked. The town was for the most part in ruins, and just before the brigade arrived the town-hall had been blown up by a clock-bomb (or time-bomb) : in it, in fact, a small advance-party had its quarters along with the rear-party of the departing brigade and with several French civilians of note : luckily very few of them were in the building when the bomb exploded. Harry wandered about the fallen as well as the partly-demolished houses : the traces of human habitation and domesticity fascinated him, and he would amuse himself by trying to piece together the lives of the former inmates. Greatly interested in a house that had evidently belonged to a solicitor, he rummaged among the books in a small but well-chosen library: Corneille and Racine, the select works of Voltaire, Diderot and Rousseau were there in compact editions; Hugo, Vigny and Musset; some of the novels of George Sand, Flaubert and Maupassant; Cherbuliez and Bordeaux appeared to be the most recent of the French novelists, Sully Prudhomme of the poets, Rostand of the dramatists; Renan and Taine were well represented. English literature supplied a complete Shakespeare, a Byron, three or four of Scott's novels, a *David Copperfield*, a *Vanity Fair*, all in the original. German, again in the original, furnished a nice edition of Goethe's *Faust* and Schiller's *William Tell*. Even Latin: especially did Harry notice a history of philosophy written in that language by a German scholar; and Greek: there was a serviceable edition of the Odyssey. In addition to these, he saw a number of law-books, some of which dated back to the Sorbonne days of their owner. But when he became depressed with the sight of so many ruined houses, he walked among the gardens of the larger residences on the outskirts of the town; hardly one of these better-class dwellings remained standing. In the long, narrow fruit and vegetable gardens at their rear, Harry lingered over a bed of strawberries, discerned a few plums that others had missed, sat beneath a shady tree in the cool sweet air of the evening: the houses he investigated when he had a free afternoon, the gardens he reserved for the hours after tea. He would gaze at the ruins, glance about at the fruit trees on either hand, and look beyond at the undulating meadow-lands that girt Bapaume on all sides. Fields that, now supporting no stock, looked like a sea of waving grass, streaked here and there with wild flowers. Some days, of course, he had neither the time nor the inclination for these gentle pleasures; the men were kept in good training with fatigues, parades, manœuvres around Riencourt-lez-Bapaume, and route-marches, one of which was by Biefvillers, Achiet-le-Grand, and Grévillers; the staff-captain was stung with the desire for all kinds of kit-inspections, will-makings, and other follies. "He has an idea that men must be kept on the *qui vive*; that they mustn't enjoy themselves too much; in short that we should be harassed like those poor devils of Tommies," said one old soldier, a friend of Harry's. From Bapaume the brigade moved to Renescure, situated roughly thirty miles behind the line and about six from St. Omer, and there they remained for the greater part of August and the first fortnight of September. The weather actually improved on its former glories. The staff-captain went on leave. There were several manœuvres, a brigade-parade and a divisional march-past (in each case Earl Haig was "the big noise"), but no long route-marches. On the other hand, games were encouraged. At Brigade-Headquarters, a great deal of cricket was played: observers against snipers; signallers and orderly-room staff against combined observers and snipers; a representative eleven against the field-ambulance; and so forth. Not far away ran a large swift-flowing canal, which attracted bathers on many a blazing afternoon. The village was not in the least exciting, but a good canteen kept one well supplied in the extras to which one considers oneself entitled when so far behind the line. One night, however, they received a most unpleasant surprise. The observers were asleep in a big barn, which stood within fifty yards of the moat surrounding a small château (occupied by the officers). A loud explosion awakened them. The majority thought it was a large bomb, perhaps half a mile away. Four minutes later—the interval separating all the seventeen shells fired in the vicinity that night—a deafening crash and a terrific vibration made them jump almost out of their skins; clods of earth were heard to fall. Everyone then realised that this was the beginning of a bombardment by a long-distance gun. The second shell had fallen a hundred yards away, the next two were not so close, but in the same line. They knew that unless "Fritz" deflected the gun a point, they might expect a shell to drop very near. In war, as in peace, a little knowledge is a dangerous thing, but expert knowledge is sometimes torture. They hoped that the direction would be changed; they counted the minutes; they held themselves taut, with, maybe, an unspoken prayer at their heart. A tremendous yet curiously muffled roar: the barn swaying and shivering: stones and clods hurtling through the air, thudding into the courtyard, popping into the midden, rattling on the roof (several coming through): no one hurt. "My God!" cried an Atheist; "Hell!" shouted an Agnostic; "Damn and blast!" muttered a good Christian; "The bloody bastard!" exclaimed a "tough"; "Holy Mary!" groaned a devout Roman Catholic. The shell had fallen into the moat, fully forty yards from the barn. It blew a pump right out of the water. The château, which, built of bricks, stood only twenty yards from the point of incidence, rocked and tottered, but remained unharmed. The general impression was that there could be no closer shave than this, and, in truth, the next shell descended two hundred yards away; of the rest none came nearer, while some fell half a mile away. The village escaped altogether. It was the first burst of all that went nearest to killing anybody: the edge of the hole lay ten yards from a cottage, which lost part of its roof but none of its peasant inhabitants; they, in fact, took a pride in their perilous distinction and preened themselves on their precedence over the military. The cavities were, on the average, fourteen feet deep and eighteen across. The men, feeling that they had had their turn, heaved a sigh of relief. Some days later, Harry departed on leave, which he began one glorious evening by walking to St. Omer and which he spent in London, Birmingham and Torquay.

When he returned to the section, it was to a camp near Poperinghe (known to the majority of soldiers as "Pop"): he had missed a "stunt" by a few days, nor did he regret his absence: to be perfectly honest, he was vastly relieved. On the way up, he had stopped several days at a dull village where the skeleton-brigade was encamped. This was the first time that his division adopted the practice (which was made obligatory) of leaving in reserve, from all battalions and during each engagement, a small number of men and officers representative of every branch of activity, riflemen, bombers, signallers, and so forth. A sound idea, soundly executed: in the skeleton, each limb contained one or two of the men wearing a metal *A* in the middle of their regimental colours: these were the "Anzacs," a term applied to all who had seen active service on Gallipoli; as early as September, 1917, they constituted a very small minority, while at the end of the war the infantry battalions of the first Australian Division could not have had more than forty, those of the Second more than fifty of their "veterans" (in many English battalions even fewer "originals" survived, for they had the advantage of longer service), and the number would have been much smaller were it not that many of these survived thanks only to a lucky job held for part of the time at some headquarters.

Soon after Harry rejoined his section, they moved from Reninghelst, *via* Dickebusch, to Ypres, where they expected to be bombed again. For at the hutments near Reninghelst, they had been bombed about ten o'clock one night with those deadly little "grass-cutters." Two dropped in the camp, the first hitting nobody, the second wounding six that, on the first burst, had foolishly stood up instead of lying flat. When they stopped a night near Dickebusch, bombs fell close by. Yet at Ypres nothing happened. They were billeted in the spacious barracks, badly battered in places but still affording tolerable shelter. In late September, 1917, the town was not such a heap of ruins as it was to become later, but the Germans had already done signal damage with artillery fire; an interesting old place to look round, and offering something to drink—if one knew where to look for it. The next day they walked rapidly along the Menin Road and off to the left. After a long stretch of dismal country, torn up by shells, they came to Brigade Headquarters in a rectangular block-house of German structure, large enough to house the whole headquarters staff. The observers carried on their work from behind and outside, standing in a hollow against the rearward wall and looking over the top. After being in a week they had a night's rest two miles further back in the huge Canadian Dugout, which had been constructed on the catacomb-system and could, at a pinch, hold two thousand men; there were bunks of an incredible hardness for a couple of hundred. It was very damp and had a peculiarly strong earthy smell. From the two entrances, themselves at the bottom of a deep trench, steps descended some thirty feet; there were several long parallel corridors intersected by numerous short galleries; very small rooms were set on either side of the corridors. The whole place as cheerless as it was interesting: rather weird were the dully glistening walls, the unusual echoes, the impression of complete detachment from all natural things, the feeling that down there one had nothing to do with green fields, little to do even with war in its more strenuous moments. One got a feeling of incompleteness and littleness: life seemed to have become pulseless, timeless: one might be a gnome in a city of gnomes. It was almost with relief that the observers went back to their post, where they remained a few days longer. Out for a week at Vlamertynghe and in for a fortnight, this time in a small round blockhouse half a mile to the right of the first and thus, though at some distance, directly facing Paschendaele Ridge. Out once more for a week (during which Harry was sent with some papers to Army headquarters at the pleasant town of Cassel), and in for about ten days: again in the large blockhouse, which they preferred, since they had been obliged to sleep outside the other; in the smaller, only the officers could occupy the one room. In this area, "Jerry" frequently used gas, mostly conveyed in those shells which burst so quietly, so gently, to emit the sickly-sweet vapour that caused a speedy donning of masks. One came to listen hard for the raucously absurd but penetrating sound of the Klaxon that announced: *Gas*. These shells popping all round made observing a picturesque but extremely difficult job; several fell into the little dug-outs in which the men slept when they were at the smaller *blockhaus* (commonly called a "pillbox"), and often, while there, the observers thought that they were sure to have a few coming through the very large opening in the frontward wall of their post, itself a kind of room with a door at the side, a covering of cement, and a floor level with the top of the mound from which the visible part of the structure arose, the officers' quarters being below the ground. During this occupation of the Ypres front, the weather was foul. The pock-marked surface of this stricken land became sodden, all the holes being filled with water: and walking along the slippery duck-boards on a pitch-black sleety night, with pools alongside (or even underneath) deep enough to drown a heavily-laden man, demanded unremitting patience, care, and alertness: one cursed the Very lights and the bursting shells, for after the sudden brightness one seemed for a moment to be moving in a sea of perfect blackness: often one had to feel one's way with one's feet. Felipé, it appeared, once slipped into a shell-hole; his language was so torrid that he crawled out looking much drier than might have been expected.

At the beginning of December, the Observers' Section had a week's spell at Steenwerck, a favourite billet some distance from the front. As during the previous periods behind the line, Harry went to see his old pal, whose service remained unbroken except by furlough. Felipé was, however, one of the earliest Australians to obtain leave to Paris, where, in the dead of winter, he had what, with an unusual paucity of phrase, he described afterwards to Harry as " a hell of a good time " ; in amplification, he explained that he had eaten like a king, visited the music halls and variety shows with the assiduity of " a first-nighter," and risen very late in the morning. " Why so late ? " asked Harry. " My dear fellow, the question is indiscreet. Suffice it to say that she had dark hair, a svelte figure, an expressive face, and that hint of russet brown in the neck which, as I have told you before, always pleases me. She spoke very little English and I even less French, but in essentials we hit it off to perfection."

About the 9th of December, the Section went on post in the Messines section of the Armentières front for a solid month, uninterrupted except for twenty-four hours' " leave " during which they marched some five miles to get a bath (moisture was also applied internally, several singing and stumbling as they cheerfully walked back again) and slept quietly till eight o'clock, when they resumed their steady observation of the allotted sector, their close examination of the front trench with occasional sharp glances at the approaches thereto, their tabulation of artillery-fire, and their attempts to determine the full meaning of the various lights employed by the enemy. In this last, they often came near to unravelling the multi-coloured skein, when, to their disgust, the significance of the lights was changed. In their other activities, however, they succeeded very much better; thanks were ironically due to the excellent Zeiss telescope which, appreciably superior to the British article supplied by ordnance, their corporal had found in a German dug-out during a small advance made in March, 1917. They observed for their own infantry brigade and reported straight to headquarters. From December, 1917, onwards they always, when it was practicable, had a field-telephone laid from the post to the brigade advance orderly-room. Sometimes they ate and slept in, or right against, the post, at others they lived from half to three-quarters of a mile behind it. If they observed from a blockhouse or from an established post (the latter, which they had only once, would necessarily be disguised and very strongly built), they naturally slept there. More often the post was extremely simple and frail, being a mere cubby-hole let into a trench, usually at the end of a short sap made especially for the purpose and running off from a communication-trench, therefore without any such movement near it as would attract the notice of the enemy, and therefore safer; this post would have an aperture sufficient for the free play of a telescope, would hold two persons and generally contain a rough seat. From April, 1918, until the Armistice, they observed either from a modest post of this kind or from the bank of a sunken road or again from an improvised hole in the ground. The last mentioned had obviously to be on an eminence. Excavated at night or behind a bank of mist, it would be about three feet wide, six long, and seven deep, with a step left for the observer and with a natural seat large enough for his companion on duty and for the telephone ; the displaced earth was scattered so that no aviator would notice it ; a small disguised parapet, with a gap (arranged if possible under a live bush—or a dead one if circumstances did not permit of the former) for the telescope. If it were a blockhouse or established post, there might be only one observer on duty, but two were preferred ; and he or they remained for two hours. If the post were some distance from the billet and there were little danger of detection, two men went on duty for three hours ; but if the danger were considerable, they remained for four.

This period on the Armentières front was interesting. They faced Warneton. The Germans became very lively at times, and twice the observers had to run the gauntlet of a five-nine bombardment on their way to the post. Once they were forced to leave it for a whole night and to carry on from a concrete dug-out eighty yards to the right : when they returned to the official position next morning with the telephone, they found several disquietingly large fragments of a shell buried in the floor and the seat. The wood which concealed their billet was shelled three or four times, one " whizz-bang " dropping just outside, others within a few yards of the sand-bag hut. Yet they lived comparatively well. For the first time (you may be sure that they urged this precedence on their officer, who managed to make it an institution) they had a special cook ; they slept, some in bunks, two on the rough table on which they ate their meals ; they had a daily ration of rum, much appreciated in that cold weather. The days were chilly, the nights freezing, but the winter of 1917-18 was much drier as well as less cold than that of 1916-17, which will always stand out in the memory of those who passed it in France. On Christmas day each man received one of those excellent plum-puddings bought with the Red Cross funds, and, in addition to the ordinary meat-ration, every two men had a Maconochie between them—a Maconochie nicely warmed is not to be despised; some of them had gone easy with the previous day's portion of rum in order to have the more for "this festive occasion" (as the corporal, fond of journalese, described it); and both British and Germans abstained from anything more than a very perfunctory "hate." During the last week of this long turn in the trenches, several of the section got leave to Paris; this meant that only one man could be on a post at a time. In the day, this was no hardship, but at night, from eight till eight, two observers put in twelve hours between them, in a period of three hours, the one off duty sleeping in a shelter about forty yards away. In case of accidents, both went up together and, when the relief arrived in the morning, back together. The first night, Harry was on duty; he and his companion decided for a comfortable though flimsy shelter as against a rather uncomfortable but very solid-looking one; several five-nines dropped nearby in the early morning, and, as they left for billet and breakfast, they saw that the solid "possie" had been flattened level with the ground; with a mutual glance of thankfulness, they hurried away feeling that they needed something warm to dispel the added chill.

After this long and exacting period of observation, the section (in common with the rest of the brigade) had four weeks out of the line. At first in huts, they then marched during two bitter days to a château standing almost exactly half way between Armentières and the sea. No visits to Felipé, for the corporal had at last obtained a release from France: from early January to the end of March he would give instruction in a machine-gun school on Salisbury Plains. If ever a man deserved to go away, it was he, for he had been in every single engagement for two years and four months. Yet even in England he struck a patch of bad luck, as Harry learnt, at the beginning of March, from one of his delightful letters : some careless fellow had shot himself with the machine-gun that Felipé used during instruction : he was called on to give evidence and, somewhat under a cloud, to explain how the accident could have arisen : genuinely sorry for the mishap, in not the slightest degree his fault, he nevertheless resented the attitude of the officer conducting the enquiry : indignantly, he justified himself in a terse and caustic manner, and, on being told that he was acquitted of neglect, he exclaimed : " A machine-gun is not fool-proof, and I protest against the gratuitous suspicion from which, evidently, I have had to clear myself. Is my good name to be tainted merely because I happen to have been in charge ? " The officer, somewhat startled but entirely convinced, replied : " All right, corporal, you are acquitted without the usual injunction to be more careful in future."

Early in February, 1918, Harry obtained six days' leave to Paris. He picked up his passport and railway ticket at Brigade Headquarters one afternoon at five o'clock and walked the three miles to Steenvoorde. In winter it is a dreary, monotonous district thereabouts. Properly speaking, his leave did not commence until the next morning, when a leave train was to depart from that town at about six and go to Calais, where the men would catch the regular afternoon train to Paris. But he was always willing to take a risk: he thought that by "wangling" his way, he might be able to reach Paris by noon instead of at seven o'clock. He began well by travelling on an English engine as far as Hazebrouck, that rather uninteresting town which, when Steenvoorde could no longer be used as the rail-head for some time after the second German offensive of 1918, became a very important military point, as "Jerry" recognised by honouring it with heavy shells. But there he stuck: he heard that nothing would run in the required direction till that leave-train stopped to take on more men. By discreet enquiries, he discovered that he might possibly be able to pass the night at an English depôt about two thousand yards from the station. He found the orderly-room after being challenged at the point of a bayonet by the conscientious Tommy on sentry-go. The reception by the clerk was chilly, but he used his most persuasive manner and "put it all over" the worthy cockney, who finally said: "If you go to the hut on the left of the court-yard, you'll find an orderly, who will show you where you can sleep."

"Might be just as well if you gave me a chit?"

He was given it. The orderly stared when it was handed to him, but, like a true English soldier, asked no questions. A rough bunk with plenty of blankets was Harry's lot: much more than he had expected. Having told the orderly when his train was to leave and after genially hinting that it might be worth his while to have a cup of tea and some "grub" ready for him, he slept the sleep of the man who knows how to look after himself. He awoke at the orderly's touch, and, having washed (he had to break the ice to get at the water), he ate the rough but ample meal placed before him: the Tommy was delighted when a five-franc note tickled his ready palm. Off to the station. The train was packed, the journey decidedly uncomfortable as far as Calais, but as everyone was in excellent spirits the talk proved highly amusing. Before taking the train at Calais, Harry made a hearty and savoury meal at the station-restaurant. From the Gare du Nord in Paris they travelled by motor-vans to the leave-depôt, where they received an excellent meal, general hints as to how to pass an agreeable holiday, a lurid account of the remarkable charms and the infinitely more remarkable dangers that would be incurred in any acquaintance with French prostitutes, and a warning against the promiscuous cultivation of friendship with the Parisian *midinettes*. A list of the addresses of some cheap, reliable and respectable hotels was given to each man. Harry chose one in what he knew to be an interesting and central quarter of Paris. He arranged only to sleep and breakfast there, so that he might wander about and eat wherever the spirit moved him and his purse allowed him; Felipé had thoughtfully sent him a loan of a couple of pounds. On his first day and several times afterwards, he visited the big "leave hotel" in the Place de la République, where he obtained a bath and clean linen. He usually set out at half-past ten (for he rose late) and strolled about the boulevards. Having on the first day lunched at the Restaurant Boulant in the

Boulevard Montmartre and found that the food was excellent, he continued to go there for his lunch at one o'clock and to sit at the same table overlooking the street. As the weather was bitterly cold, he wisely refrained from visits to Versailles and Fontainebleau. Nor did he see many of the " sights " even in Paris : after idling on the boulevards for a while after lunch, he would generally go to a cinema ; then to his hotel for a rest and a smoke. After dinner (he varied the restaurant for this meal), he would " do " a theatre, a music-hall, or a variety show, the Folies Bergères amusing him considerably except when the cynicism became mere vulgarity : he was one of those who do not mind how " fast " a joke may be, if it is really witty and not disgusting. In short he had a quiet, restful and thoroughly pleasant holiday and a mild flirtation with an English girl-student whom he met in the Musée Cluny and took with him to several of the evening entertainments. Back to the Observers' Section. From Calais the journey was vilely cold. Transport officers " didn't quite know " where Brigade Headquarters might be : he spent a night at Amiens till they found out. He had to retrace his route, and from this terminus he walked valiantly till he ran headquarters to earth on the outskirts of a delightful Picardy village.

At the end of February, the section returned to the Armentières front, though not to the same post. This time it was to an observation-tower built within a ruined house standing about three-quarters of a mile behind the front line. The tower was of concrete, and at its base, though somewhat lower, were a tiny dormitory constructed of concrete and containing four bunks, each large enough to hold two, and, on a level with the foot of the ladder by which one climbed to the tower and then sat on an unbacked seat with space gaping beneath, another room of the same size used as a " dining-room " for all and a dormitory for three ; the former was horribly wet, there being water a foot deep on the floor—one reached the bunks by means of heavy planks ; the latter, however, was dry —that is to say, comparatively, for while the walls glistened with moisture, the floor was no more than damp. The observation work was interesting, and, when the shells began to whistle around the tower, one could not refrain from thinking that one could support with equanimity a less positive form of excitement. When their work ended, they marched back one night to a billet eight miles distant ; their path did not lie through Armentières, but they made a slight detour in order to " have a beer " at a small café on the outskirts. A small room filled with soldiers, smoking, drinking, talking noisily and playfully courting the two sturdy, cheerful French girls who stayed on when most of the inhabitants had left ; a heartening, lively scene, the more pleasant when one rarely sees either beer or women. At last they tore themselves away and tramped to their destination. After changing billets twice and moving more or less in a circle, they occupied one not far from Armentières. These huts, according to a practice that became common about the middle of 1917, were protected by strong sandbag walls, with a gap opposite the door : these sufficed against all but heavy bombs, except of course when " Fritz " scored a direct hit. While Harry was at this camp, Felipé returned to his battalion looking much the better for his sojourn in England. He was so energetic that, departing from his usual practice, he visited the Observers twice and set the whole section roaring with his account of the machine-gun school.

Late in March came the famous German offensive. The reports sounded so grave that the Observers did not believe them, but the official *communiqués* (posted regularly, throughout the war, on the battalion, brigade, and other notice-boards) confirmed the rumours. Many of the Australian troops were rushed to the Somme, the situation being so serious that they actually went part of the way, by St. Pol and Doullens, in trains : a conclusive indication of urgency, so far, at least, as Australian troops were concerned ; rarely too did they embus. They detrained at Amiens, itself close to the deepest thrust of the German advance. In the dawn they marched through the silent streets of this hospitable town, which remembers all British soldiers with affection and the Australians with gratitude superadded. Like Albert, Amiens often served as a point of departure, in the sense that when a battalion came into the line on this front, it usually traversed or skirted the one or the other. Harry had seen the former in the three stages of partial destruction in the summer of 1916, of a more thorough demolition (by bombs) in 1917, and of tentative repair early in 1918 : it was to suffer a further reverse before the war ended. Amiens he never knew well, despite the evening that he spent there in February 1918.

From the suburbs of Amiens they marched to a château where they remained for the rest of the day. At night, moving obliquely, they proceeded a short stage on their journey. There seemed to be some doubt as to which point of the line they were to occupy. Having halted for an afternoon and a night (during both of which "Jerry" shelled them at intervals), the brigade went into the line. While there, Harry learnt of the death of Don Wall, recently made a lieutenant: "one star, one stunt." The Observers, with a billet in the cellar of a two-storeyed, six-roomed house near an unimportant cross-roads, had a post on the shoulder of a low hill, from which they could survey at ease the enemy trench across the valley. It was rather strange to be fighting in country that several weeks before had lain well to the rear of the British line. Not far from their billet stood a Y.M.C.A. hut, partly demolished by a German shell: they took a dozen books from the small library, enough to occupy them during the three May weeks passed in this vicinity; the Brigade Snipers, who occupied part of the same building, had also laid in a store. The billet stood on flat land, with a tiny hamlet a hundred yards to the right and to the front a sugar-refinery at some distance but directly in front. (A cellar of this refinery was later used by the section as a billet.) A village situated on a small river lay a mile to the right, and to the left of their billet was the low hill on which, at the forward part, stood their post and on the rearward, the Brigade Headquarters. It was the Ribemont and Morlancourt district. To reach the post, they walked first about five hundred yards along a road and then, from a landmark, four hundred yards at a precise right angle. These details may sound unimportant, but when a post stands on the brow of a hill, fully visible to any German furnished with a telescope, when there are no landmarks on that brow, and when the pit constituting the post cannot be detected more than twenty yards away in full daylight, it is necessary not only to choose the exact route that, while the sun is up, will afford the most cover in the way of undulations, but also, in case those on watch should be killed or hurt, to enable the relief, even on the darkest or the wildest night, to walk straight to the spot. When they discarded the post and dug another, six hundred yards further from the billet, they had merely to follow the wire of the telephone that they insisted should be supplied : in a sector like this, where " Jerry " had chafed exceedingly at being held up by " those damned Aussies," it was advisable that the observers should immediately communicate all suspicious activities. It was a pretty lively district, even then ; afterwards it became much too warm. In those clear, sunny days of May, " when only man was a blot on the landscape," it seemed an almost unimaginable crime that war should be waged in this fair country side. Then a wholly unexpected shell would crash on the road outside the billet or near the post. Sometimes at night, " Jerry " decided that he would put down a barrage on the front trench or on one of the roads or on the hill occupied by the observers ; he would " go mad " for half an hour.

At the end of May the Brigade came out of the line for a short spell. The first stop was at Querrieu, the delightful little village that adjoins Pont-Noyelles : two hamlets that look as one. Harry little realised that this was the last time that he would use an observation post. Little too, did he think that, when he ran across Felipé one day just outside the billet at the cross-roads, he was seeing him for the last time.

Harry, never very strong, had been gradually becoming a serious debility case: for two months he could walk for more than four miles only with the greatest difficulty; he collapsed three or four times on long route marches. But extreme debility, as tenacious as it was pronounced, would not have sufficed to take him away when men were badly needed. Two days after he left the line, he reported one morning at eleven (he had from five o'clock endured three hours of sentry-go at the entrance of the Querrieu château temporarily utilised as headquarters) to the M.O., who sent him away immediately with a serious attack of tonsilitis. He went again to Rouen, this time to an American hospital. The tonsilitis disappeared in due course, but trench-fever had set in. He was sent to England—and to one of the most delectable of places: Stratford-on-Avon. When he was convalescent, he visited Warwick and Leamington Spa. Late in July, he reported to headquarters in Horseferry Road, Westminster; the doctor asked him if he felt quite fit to go on furlough: "No, I'm much too weak. Ought to have a fortnight in a convalescent-camp."

"Rubbish, man! you'll do. Leave will set you up."

So off he went. Four days later he was admitted to hospital in Bristol with a nasty relapse of trench-fever. After a month there and three weeks in a camp on Salisbury Plains, he finished his furlough in London and Scotland.

Even when he returned from leave, he was still debilitated. He was kept at Sutton Veny, near Warminster, where he helped his country by acting as orderly-clerk at divisional headquarters. There he remained until several days before Christmas, when he sailed for Australia in an old German cargo-boat that took an unconscionable time to reach Brisbane. At the city he had left nearly four years previously, he received his discharge: one of the numerous men who had served without a stain on their name, with quiet distinction but with no decorations except those indicative of long service. For himself, Harry did not regret the absence of a medal; but that Felipé, who had "done his bit" so long, so gallantly, so continuously in the front line, was never decorated—this made his blood boil. The corporal of machine-gunners was killed in September, 1918. A mutual friend wrote to Harry: "Dear Onslow, I have some very bad news for you. Yes, Phillips. I saw him just before the stunt at . . . began. 'It's the end this time', he said: 'I've had a long run.' I reassured him. 'I *know*,' he replied with a strange light in his eyes. As we shook hands, he added: 'I want you to do one thing for me. Remember me to Onslow. I would like you to tell him about it.' Poor devil! He got a machine-gun bullet through the brain soon after the attack commenced. Yours sincerely, Fred Williams." Felipé's fatalism probably resulted from the fact that when he was sent to Rouen in August with a slight wound, he missed a general evacuation of the wounded to England by being away somewhere with a book at the time the senior medical officer came round; he had written to Harry soon afterwards: "I've missed my chance. Fate never forgives a thing like that," he said.

"Well," mused Harry, when the pain of the blow had eased, "he died like the fine soldier that he would have hated to be called. A true man, and a wonderful friend. God! How I shall miss him."

A TALE OF THREE CITIES

A TALE OF THREE CITIES

THE Modern History Board decided, after considerable discussion, to allow Douglas Stevenson to submit, for the purposes of an advanced degree, a thesis on " The Social Interpenetration of France and England during the reign of Queen Anne." This was in 1921, in the middle of the Michaelmas Term. Stevenson had taken a brilliant " first " in History at the University of Bristol earlier in the same year, when his father decided to send him to Oxford.

Thither he proceeded with a due sense of modesty, for he knew that many a student with a " first " in Classics or English or Modern History or what-not from some provincial or colonial university might well fail, after the two years required in this case for a B.A., to get anything better than a " third " or at most a " second " ; while of the advanced students (with good reputations elsewhere), a number fell short of the standard exacted for a B.Litt. or Ph.D. Douglas Stevenson was aiming at the lesser degree, but it is to be remarked both that he was prepared to spend two full years on it and that in those days the B.Litt. was not a stepping stone to a Ph.D. ; it was a wholly independent degree, usually taken by one who could not give to his work the time required for the more ambitious " letters." In 1921 it was mainly the extent of the subject which determined the degree, now it is rather the difficulty and importance which settle the matter.

The nature of Douglas's thesis meant that he would have to work in London and Paris as well as at Oxford. He was not wholly unaware of this during the fortnight in which he debated alternate subjects with his father. The subject finally chosen appealed to them both. " The extra expense, my boy, is considerable. You must therefore go to a college where the fees are comparatively low." He decided that he would attach himself to the Non-Collegiate Delegacy, where he knew several old Bristol men.

He was vaguely amused at having to go through another matriculation ceremony. A group of young men clothed in garments that must be either black or noticeably dark and wearing stiff collars with white ties—the regulation dress for Oxford students on all official occasions—may present little to delight the eye of the sensation-monger, but the effect is pleasing, for the short gown resembles a cape in that it is both neat and romantic, while the mortar-board is not worn but carried like a prayer-book. The ceremony itself, with its relics of mediævalism and its gift of the *Excerpta Statutorum* (or " rules and regs.," as they are more often called), is at once impressive and interesting; indeed, one can say as much of all the Oxford ceremonies, in some of which the comic element is supplied by the proctors. One feels rather sorry at times for these two junior officers.

Douglas aimed to divide his year approximately as follows : of the eight weeks in a term, he had to put in only six at Oxford, and he rarely exceeded the six, except in the summer when it would be difficult to find a spot more delightful than this fascinating old city ; at the end of each term (as he kept it), he would go to London for a lunar month; then home for ten days at Christmas, a week at Easter, three weeks in "the long"; the rest of the time he would pass in Paris. He intended to work really hard for nine-tenths of the year: and, strange to say, he did not suffer his intentions so to stray on the primrose path that he lagged behind: if, apart from the joy of work, he derived much pleasure and some excitement from life, he did so after his reading was finished for the day; or if he took a few days off in London or Paris, he made up for lost time in Clifton.

His parents lived at Sion Hill, overlooking the magnificent gorge, within two minutes' walk of the Suspension Bridge, and opposite Nightingale Wood. "Your residential lines are cast in pleasant places," remarked an envious student from Wolverhampton. To his credit, he loved his native place. Whenever he felt that he needed a "breather," he strolled over the Clifton Downs, which invariably dispersed the cobwebs and restored him to freshness and equanimity; the stories of smugglers' dens (more authentic than the majority of such tales) pleased his fancy. He was regarded as an authority on local traditions, in which Bristol and its suburbs are rich. But he displeased the city councillors by exploding several Chatterton myths. Nor was it only Bristol and Clifton that had engaged his historical interests when he was an undergraduate, for he sometimes visited the utterly charming and the agreeably cultured city of Bath, now shorn of the social splendour that made it prosperous in the eighteenth and early nineteenth centuries, but still—partly, perhaps, on account of that "decadence"—an alluring place: it is one of those to which (like Oxford, Cambridge,

Winchester, and Tunbridge Wells) one would like to retire when " the day's work " is done; and not one of the less fortunate class in which one would gladly live only in the sunny half of the year, such as York and Chester.

At Oxford, Douglas Stevenson lived in " digs." He was the only undergraduate (he could not at first realise that though he had an honours degree, he was an undergraduate) in a small house in James Street, just off the Iffley Road. In the first term, before he knew whether his subject would be approved, he went to various lectures. His tastes being catholic, he did not confine himself to courses in Modern History. He enjoyed the lectures of men like Gilbert Murray and Walter Raleigh, both of whom have done so much to keep alive the Oxford tradition of culture and learning, of charm and originality, for, like Cambridge, Oxford sets power and originality of intellect far before mere information. The standard of knowledge and learning is extremely high, and erudition may ensure respect and a " second " : but esteem is reserved for the man who has a notable mind of his own, and only he who, to erudition, adds such a mind, can obtain a " first " in the examinations or a post on the staff.

There is an intellectual atmosphere at the two senior universities of England which brings forth the latent qualities of the students much more extensively, profoundly and subtly than organised system or thoroughgoing efficiency will ever do elsewhere. Moreover, if one examines procedure and has some " inside " knowledge of administration, one comes to the conclusion that the organisation at Oxford and Cambridge is not inferior but superior to that of any other university in Great Britain ; much less talk is made about it ; and it retains a more pleasant, more human element. There is a liberality and open-mindedness about the dons and the examinations of Oxford and Cambridge which, with certain charming exceptions, are represented in the other universities largely by the men from those two places ; the curricula in London and the provinces are more rigid, as can be readily seen in the Law, Theology, English, Classics and Modern History courses. Douglas Stevenson sometimes heard it said that the lure of the British Museum Library would draw increasingly large numbers of the best academic brains to London ; "But," he asked one student who advanced this statement, "does that bear examination ? Only those whose work may be described as research and erudition will find that they are forced to dig in that wonderful mine ; of these scholars there must be very few who, in the long university vacations, cannot spare the necessary time to go to London ; moreover, if they cannot, in the provincial universities, find leisure for private work during term, it is pretty certain that in London (where members of the various college staffs have more lecturing) they will find even less. If the excellence of a university teacher, apart from the *sine qua non* of a certain ability to teach, depended on erudition alone, and not on erudition plus an original and powerful mind, then and then only would the British Museum Library turn the scale." In the Arts, Oxford and Cambridge will always retain their marked superiority, and they do not in the least mind that they have no medical degree, no school of tropical medicine like that at Liverpool, that the primacy in certain kinds of science belongs to Manchester, in certain others to London. The student-life in the two university-towns, a life that will always attract the best qualities of youth, plays a tremendous part, too, in the development of the undergraduates ; the corporate life elsewhere is an ideal, not a fact ; and it were a sorry jest to compare the residential halls of cities like London and Manchester with a college like Trinity or King's at Cambridge, Magdalen or Christ Church at Oxford.

Douglas, as a student of history, had always been keenly interested in the prestige enjoyed by Oxford and Cambridge ; now that he was an undergraduate of the former, he studied it more closely. When he was in London, he stayed at a students' hostel ; when in Paris, at a *pension* frequented by foreign as well as French students : he made a practice of inveigling them (it was easy enough) into talking about their own universities : having done this for two years, he was, at the end of his course, thoroughly saturated in the features, characteristics and tendencies of the British universities as seen by students.

In his more legitimate studies, he made satisfactory progress. It was independent work, in which he had to find his own way about : he was saved from gross mistakes by his supervisor, one of Oxford's greatest scholars, a man whose remarkable eminence in three subjects was equalled only by his luminous insight into general thought, by his originality of outlook and expression, by his stimulating, provocative and suggestive lecturing, tutoring, and supervising : one who carried his immense learning with engaging lightness and a pretty wit. Every student, young or mature, who went to Dr. A'Jacy esteemed himself fortunate, admired his tutor's erudition, was captivated by his open-mindedness and dazzled by his originality; and all tried to give of their best. By A'Jacy as much as by any don, the finest men of the present century have been moulded. It is this which constitutes his greatest value, although his name as a scholar will live as long as Oxford exists. Naturally, he has his detractors, who, envying the range and profundity of his knowledge, talk darkly of that mastery of no trade which characterises the Jack of all; those who are more kindly disposed sometimes regret that he has not devoted all his energies to one branch of enquiry, and his best friends and most fervent admirers admit that, as regards learning, what is extension's gain is concentration's deplorable loss. Had he definitely taken up any one of his three subjects, he might have had any post in England in that subject: but while such a step would have undoubtedly brought him greater fame and the likelihood of a more enduring place in the intellectual history of mankind, his defection from unity has, probably to a considerable extent, increased his influence over "the young men": few, even among his enemies, have denied that his influence is beneficial. Hatred of sciolism, readiness to work hard in order to throw light on obscure points, the due subordination of knowledge (however great) to the matter in hand, denunciation of cant and insincerity, distrust of partiality, a fearless honesty of purpose, the ineradicable belief that social problems are worthy the steel of the finest intellects, the desire to reach the heart of a subject, the arts of subtle argument and luminous exposition, the human touch that strikes a responsive chord in all men, unobtrusive affability, an unassuming love of one's fellows, a deep respect for intellect, a humble reverence for the divine: these qualities distinguish the best of his old students.

Douglas saw his supervisor at the beginning of his studies and thereafter only at the end of each term. Nominally he went for an hour, but actually he stayed two or more. He made the most of those visits and contrived to lengthen them by engaging in discussions: it is perhaps a tribute to some small ability that he succeeded. Now that he is on the highroad to an important professorship in History, he recognises his unrepayable debt to his old friend: it is to him, in fact, that he owes his gift of keeping his very considerable erudition in the background while he employs it to illuminate and simplify a subject; to him that he owes the rapid development of his power of visualising periods, discarding (though not forgetting) the secondary details, and presenting a masterly summary exposition; to him also he traces the aim characterising all great historians: to understand and make clear the general movement in the history of a nation, an idea, an influence: to show the soul and mind functioning amid the welter of political and social events.

Perhaps Douglas derived the more benefit from Oxford that he was twenty-five when he "came up." He had served two years with the British Army in France and Belgium, received his discharge in June, 1918, because of a serious illness, and commenced his university course at Bristol in October of the same year. France had matured him and set him seriously thinking and observing: to watch a great nation fighting for its rights, to examine it at close quarters, was no bad beginning of an adequate, human study of history; to have fought and suffered and rejoiced with all sorts and conditions of men was an invaluable aid to the understanding of mass-movements and mass-psychology. The rough edges were knocked off at Bristol by a dear old professor, who did much to help him. And now at Oxford he revelled in its peculiar ambience, availed himself whole-heartedly of its vast historical and literary wealth and its many-sided culture, responded keenly and sensitively to its intellectual and æsthetic provocations, made a point of listening attentively to all the lecturers in the History school and to some in Classics, in two or three modern languages, and in English and Philosophy. He enjoyed the scholarly and attractive historianship of Firth, the vitalising, fruitfully modern treatment of Greek history by Seymour, the charm of Pickard-Cambridge, the erudition and method of Rudler, the independent and individual continuance of the Raleigh tradition by Gordon (this in Douglas's second year), the learning and excellent taste of Nichol Smith, the combative brilliance of Schiller. He met "the great men" if and when a chance offered. He belonged to, and occasionally spoke at, the Oxford Union, which drew him every session-night : took an active part in the life of his college : for why should the Non-Collegiate Delegacy not be called a college ? He was a member of its historical society (familiarly known as "the D.K.") and its debating society, while its literary society (the Apollo) liked to receive him as a visitor, for he usually had some interesting comments to make; indeed, while he remained a stalwart of "the D.K." he became a subscribing member of the

Apollo in his second term. On Saturday nights, there was a "hall-dinner" served in the junior common room,—one of the numerous features that the Censor introduced so successfully to strengthen the corporate life of this non-residential college,—and Douglas attended two or three times a term; he found it agreeable and convenient to dine there and stay on for "the debater." He was frequently to be seen occupying a comfortable chair in the spacious and pleasant library of the Delegacy; the quietness helped him to work. Although he read much at "the Radder" and "the Bodder," he found the former a little strenuous—a British Museum Reading Room on a reduced scale: and when he could get the books he wanted, he preferred the airy room at the Delegacy. As his thesis was historical, he often saw the Censor, who, in addition to being a charming English gentleman, was an indefatigable and sympathetic administrator and a witty lecturer with an unusually clear exposition. When he went for advice, Douglas always found him helpful and, no matter how busy, always patient and affable. As he said one day to a fellow "Non-Coll": "If one didn't know how frightfully busy he was, one would suppose that the Censor asked for nothing more than the continuance of one's charming company. I sometimes tear myself away conscience-stricken. He really oughtn't to be so entertaining and sympathetic!"

In the Michaelmas and Hilary terms, Douglas Stevenson concentrated on study. Walking provided him with sufficient exercise to keep him fit, and as it was always on foot that he went into the town every morning, returned to his "digs" for lunch, and often made another trip to one of the libraries either before or after tea, he had no need for special walks. His societies and an occasional tea with friends preserved his freshness. In the Trinity term, he played regularly with the College eleven more by virtue of his good fellowship than for any merit as a cricketer. Although his army experience had taught him how to " hold his liquor," he usually went the whole term without drinking anything stronger than coffee, unless it were to " imbibe a beer " at one of his infrequent hall-dinners. The practice of drinking at the Randolph, the Mitre, the East Gate, for the sake of the thrill to be got from the possible advent of a " Prog " ; the defiant discarding of gowns in order to attract or circumvent the " bullers " (the polite designation of the University police) ; the cultivation of undesirable acquaintances :—those mild forms of excitement left him cold. It sometimes amused him to watch a " rag," and he took a genial pleasure in the exploit of that very " stout " fellow who, after a memorable climb, hung on the topmost point of the Martyrs' Memorial an object not often mentioned in polite society ; that this considerable feat was performed by the undergraduate in emulation of his father added piquancy to the prank. He delighted in the tales of two colonial friends (Rhodes Scholars and " good sports ") who seemed to have the knack of encountering odd characters. Especially an old don who would visit the public-houses on the outskirts of Oxford and, on the unwelcome irruption of " prog " or " buller " in the midst of a group of undergraduates, save the latter from a fine by a timely invitation to " have one " with him.

During his first serious visit to London, Douglas read industriously at the British Museum with occasional digressions to the Public Records Office; his hostel lay within easy walking-distance of both places. The latter offered few diversions, but the former was a constant source of covert amusement. The number of "B.M." *habitués* who talk to themselves is surprisingly large; that of queer-looking persons even larger. What some of them do there is a mystery. On the other hand, there are several readers so faithful, so regular that, even in this crowded library, they are, by common consent, privileged to occupy certain places: if an unwitting newcomer should jump one of these claims, he receives so withering, indignant and injured a glance that he feels like an interloper of the worst kind. Of these "institutions," the best known and the mildest is he who has the reputation of being one of three most learned men in Europe. Some habitual readers follow in the footsteps of Samuel Butler by using a large and abstruse tome as a pledge, or, in the face of a stern regulation, a book-rest, while others would appear to consider the reading room as a dormitory, a lounge for the post-lunch nap. Such various oddities, however, did not prevent Douglas from working hard, and, in common with most frequenters of the library, he was as much impressed by the helpfulness and courtesy of the officials as he had been at Oxford; but, unlike some students, he did not abuse that kindness. He was rather glad, however, that his work often took him into the North Library: the transition from the general reading-room thither was like leaving the bustle of Holborn for the calm of Bloomsbury Square. Even the Periodical Room was quiet, save for the abashed rustling of the agitated sheets. As for the Manuscript Room, no profane pen could render adequately its ecclesiastical calm, the awed silence, the secret pleasure of those who found themselves admitted to work there; one feels that this is a sort of initiation into the byways of learning; indeed the air of importance assumed (often, we believe, unconsciously) by the readers might lead one to suppose that this was the only road royal to academic or literary fame.

Quiet days. Yet after he had been three weeks in London, Douglas Stevenson met with an adventure that disturbed him for some time and came near to delaying his visit to Paris. He had struck up an acquaintance with a young foreigner at the Museum, had invited him along to the hostel one evening for dinner, and accepted the return. They went to a restaurant in Soho: a French place, good food, lively company. Afterwards, Douglas walked with Cardu to the latter's room. The hotel had evidently seen better days. The room, however, was a comfortable "bed-sitter." An attractive girl lay on a sofa. "Mr. Stevenson, my sister." It occurred to Douglas that the family likeness was slight. They talked on general matters. The girl knew London quite well; Cardu did not. Perhaps half an hour later—it would be about ten o'clock—Cardu picked up a letter and asked Douglas if he would mind if he slipped out to post it; "I want it to go to-night: I shall be back in a few minutes." As Corinne was pretty and charming, the young Englishman did not mind if the other were to stay away for longer. She exercised all her lures; he was inexperienced. A neatly gartered knee peeped from beneath her skirt : she looked at him with her soul in her eyes (so he thought) : he enfolded her, kissed her. Somehow, rather more than a knee became visible ; the lacy extremity of a gauze-like garment showed maddeningly. He pressed his mouth to hers. With one arm she held him fast, with the other she raised her dress even more. She tapped ever so lightly on the wall, Cardu re-entered the room to the accompaniment of her well-simulated scream. "*Il me viole!*" she cried. Douglas jumped to his feet, saw her thighs displayed and her dress disordered ; he stood aghast.

" What does this mean, Monsieur ? " demanded Cardu in a threatening voice.

" Listen, Cardu, don't be a fool! I meant no harm."

"No harm ? *On ne viole pas les jeunes filles que par plaisanterie, voyez-vous !* "

" The beast was beginning to maul me about when you so fortunately entered, Jules. I am afraid to think what might have happened if you had been any longer."

" There's a terrible mistake somewhere," asserted Douglas stoutly, his anger growing.

" It doesn't look like a mistake, Monsieur," re-joined Cardu, pointing significantly.

He was shocked and horrified to see that his clothes were somewhat disarranged. He remembered now that he had felt her hand brush against him, so swiftly, so casually that it appeared an accident ; the caress (light as thistledown) had troubled him. As he looked, so did the girl ; she gave a little shriek and covered her eyes. Douglas turned away and set his clothes in order. What was afoot ? He was not kept long in ignorance.

"Well, Monsieur," asked Cardu, "what are you going to do about it?"

"What am I going to do about it?" repeated the victim, somewhat bewildered.

"Yes." Cardu's voice cut like a knife. "The penalty for rape, Monsieur, is heavy. And then your good name," he insinuated.

Douglas thought quickly. Of course, if there were a charge brought, his name would inevitably be tarnished (the circumstantial evidence being so damning), even if he could prove his innocence. After all, what had he intended to do with the girl? Had he intended anything? No; he was carried away, and she complied. If there had been no interruption, things might have gone pretty far; why had he drunk so much at the restaurant and why had he accepted a second liqueur on reaching Cardu's room, thus inflaming his imagination? But, as he discerned in a flash, the evidence was almost too complete. He remembered that tap on the wall, slight though it was. In the second in which he was free to think about it, he had guessed that it was perhaps a ringed finger slipping against the wooden back of the sofa. He had not heard Cardu come along the passage, yet he had listened for him—for he naturally did not wish his love-making to be interrupted; the fellow must have sneaked along to the door and waited for the signal, obviously the tap. And Corinne's clothes and his: he knew jolly well that he had caused neither disarray. Damned slick work! No, he'd see them to hell rather than give in weakly. He had been a fool, but he was not an idiot. In the summer of 1917 he had been cornered in a trench by two Germans, but, by using his wits, he escaped. He didn't know how he would extricate himself from this mess. But he would try. "By the way, Cardu," he said quietly, "will you be able to prove that this is your sister? You'll have to show your papers."

"Of course she is," he snorted. "You can't bluff me like that."

"Well, I don't think she is. If the truth were known, she is probably your mistress."

"You are adding insult to injury, Monsieur!" And the girl snapped:

"You are no gentleman."

"Just at present," remarked Douglas drily, "I prefer to be a man."

Cardu and Corinne exchanged looks and several rapid phrases in French: too rapid for his unpractised ears.

"See here," exclaimed the man, "if you will give us fifty pounds, we'll let you go and say no more about it."

"Ah, blackmail! I'm afraid there's nothing doing."

"We'll see," was the retort as he produced a revolver. The bluff might have succeeded with a young, callow undergraduate such as Cardu thought Stevenson to be; the latter had said nothing about his age and military service.

"Don't be a damned fool! If you were to shoot me, you'd be captured by the police and then, *cher ami*, strung up." More signals between those two. As Cardu continued to threaten, Corinne managed to catch Douglas's arms from behind, the man leaping at him and striking him in the face. The blow and the weight from behind caused him to fall, but quick as thought he hurled himself back and fell on the girl, who struck her head on the floor and lay stunned. He freed himself violently and staggered to his feet; as he rose, Cardu struck him forcibly on the ear. He fell again. Cardu made to kick him in the ribs, but Douglas stopped the blow with his arms, got to his knees and lurched heavily forward, gripping his opponent round the waist; although somewhat dazed, he realised that he must not let go. Cardu pounded him on head and shoulders, without succeeding in loosening that grip. Douglas suddenly threw his left arm about the other's knees and simultaneously shot his fist, with all his might, to the point of his jaw. Cardu toppled back and landed on his head, definitely out of action. He lay senseless. Breathing heavily, Douglas sat a moment on the sofa, grew calm, tidied his clothes and straightened his tie. He picked up his hat and strode rapidly from the room. The porter gave him a curious glance, but half a crown stilled his doubts. Next morning, Douglas sent an anonymous letter to the police: "You might have a look at No. 17, —— Street; they are a queer lot."

A week later he went to Paris, read at the St. Geneviève Library, near which he lodged. He explored the Latin Quarter, visited a few of the sights, and tested *bière blonde*, which he considered too watery, and *bière brune*. Of the latter, he found an excellent brand (certain experts claim that it is the best in Paris) at the Café Balzar, a homely yet lively place in the rue des Ecoles, where later an American friend was to go for the excellent snails, he himself for the juicy *Chateaubriands*. He heard a Molière comedy at the Odéon and became a frequenter of the bookstalls in the galleries outside. At the Comédie Française he enjoyed some wonderful elocution in the *Cid* and in a " drame " by Dumas *fils*. He returned at Easter and watched the budding glory, the tender greens of the boulevards and the Luxembourg gardens. This time he read at the Bibliothèque Nationale.

In the summer of 1922 he went again to his *pension* in the rue St. Jacques. A building of interesting historical associations; the boarders, students of most of the European nations. The French students, however, were away for their holidays, the remaining boarders being mostly English and American. Several of the latter were agreeable, well-educated, and entertaining. He played bridge with them, sometimes in their rooms, sometimes in his. Often, too, they sallied forth together to a café, where they drank or danced. They came to frequent a small café in the Latin Quarter, near the Seine; in a room downstairs, one danced. They created a small sensation by dancing together; when Douglas returned, the following Christmas, he found that they had set a fashion. This reacted profitably on the French girls who were usually to be seen there, for they had to be more charming and alluring than ever to obtain partners and drinks.

One evening, Brough, an American friend—now an " old hand " in Paris—proposed that they should go to an " amusing " café in the St. Denis district, whither they took a taxi. " Don't expect you've been to a place like this before, Stevenson," remarked Brough as they descended. One had to ring. They were admitted. They passed through a passage into a brilliantly-lit room, with small tables and chairs around the walls, the middle unencumbered for dancing. Douglas drew a startled breath. He had not expected this. Men were sitting at the tables with drinks before them and girls on their knees. Three couples, all women, were dancing to a lively jazz tune, which was, of course, American. Every woman—the majority were French, fair and dark, with several Siamese and African girls—was stark naked. Some were natural, some were evidently artists' models. At intervals a man and a girl would disappear upstairs, where, confided Brough, were a number of small rooms furnished with little more than a rough bed ; that little more was of a significant nature. " None of them appeal to you ? " whispered Brough.

" No, thanks! " said Douglas tersely. So shameless a display of secret allurements had the effect of deadening and killing any desire that the sight was manifestly designed to arouse. The party ordered drinks ; that was obligatory. They " treated " three girls, this being their own number. Douglas pretended to understand no French and thus was free to observe. The couples danced lasciviously with suggestive movements and noises, looking provocatively at various unoccupied males. If a girl were " treated " but received no invitation to ascend, she moved off with a pout. Douglas then noted that the face of one of them was familiar. Corinne! She did not look at him as she came into the room, aglow with the embrace of a man whom he did not see except from the back. He started, pulled himself together. " Not likely to to be any trouble unless that scoundrel Cardu is with her," he reflected. He shaded his face with a distrait hand. She went to the front of the room, dispossessed the pianist of her seat, and, sitting in the simple stool, began a dainty *schottische espagnole.* The grace and affected movement of this dance seemed decidedly out of place in a café reeking with smoke, garishly lit, with the men drinking beers and wines and cocktails or jesting coarsely with the smiling women who shared the wine but mostly eschewed the beer: in a den consecrated (if one might use the word in such a connection) to the pleasures of the belly and more especially to the motions of the flesh. An exquisite step ended in a lewd gesture, a melodious chord in a hard laugh. As the music ceased, two girls, stopping in front of the strangers, bent back with supple grace until their hands touched the floor and their hips grazed the rim of the table: Brough, now "comfortable," picked up his own glass and his American companion's and dashed the contents on their gleaming skin. They resumed the upright position, looked indignant, and broke into smiles as the offender called to the nearest waiter: "*Deux verres de champagne pour ces belles filles, et vivement!*" The girls sat where they had so impudently displayed their shameless charms. Brough asked one—the prettier, as was his custom—if she were a model, "*car moi, mademoiselle, je suis peintre.*" She was—when a longer-established profession failed to bring in sufficient money. Would she not come to his studio on such a date? She would, and wrote her address in his note-book; but he did not give his. "*J'adore les blondes, surtout de belles blondes élancées comme vous!*" She smiled, tried to wheedle him upstairs, and, seeing a gentle refusal in his sparkling eyes, returned to the piano. "*Eh bien, Corinne, une Java pour nous égayer un peu!*" The wild and barbaric "Java" rang from the keys. Douglas watched the girl playing: her fine neck, her shapely back and round, enticing hips, her plump yet exquisite thighs, and her slender ankles formed a picture of which the charm was not lost on him, much as he now detested her; she swung half round to watch the swirling dancers a moment. A firm and alluring breast stood out from the profiled bust. Douglas blinked and returned to his bock. The dancers were stepping with an abandon and a verve, a rhythm and a smoothness that may have been partly due to the fact that one member of each couple was a a negress (young, supple, and masculinely handsome), and a beautiful aspect of their degraded natures was glimpsed when, forgetting the men that sat admiring them, they were possessed more and more with the spirit, the swing and the impetus of the dance; their eyes became softer, their movements discarded all aphrodisiac gestures and all impure suggestions; the joy of pure motion, the happiness of a harmless present, the memory of the best days of a far different past, and the absence of any chilling adumbration of suffering at the thought of inevitably fading attractions were vaguely inferred from a steady observation of their renewed innocence.

But for Douglas the spell was broken when from the front of the café, where he had been talking with the keeper of the door, appeared one whom, despite the change from conventional bourgeois to debauched adventurer, he recognised as Cardu. Why had he been such a fool as to remain? He had hoped that Corinne would be led away by some amorous man, but he who had descended with her was (he realised it now) Jules Cardu. The couple exchanged a few words ; the man went upstairs again as if to await her coming. After a short and carelessly-rendered fox-trot she arose, was about to set her foot on the stair, and suddenly stood as if turned to stone. Douglas knew that she had seen him. He stiffened his body as if for a blow, his heart as if for a shock. She came across to the table and halted by his side. " You here! " she hissed in English ; " you are not in London now, remember."

" So I perceive by your costume, Mademoiselle."

His smile deceived her. " Am I not pretty ? "

" As pretty as Eve," he replied. Someone else had gone to the piano, the dancing recommenced, such a dialogue attracted no attention, although Brough, at a nudge from Douglas, became quietly alert ; the third member of the party, a hefty boxer from Yale, was apprised that " something was doing."

" Will you come upstairs with me ? " she asked as she rubbed her flank against him.

" I think not, Corinne," he answered with an unconcerned laugh. At that moment, Cardu impatiently descended to look for her. He flashed into anger to see her engaged in earnest conversation with one of his own sex. "*Mon Dieu !*" he muttered, "*ce sacré Stevenson.*" He did not wish to renew acquaintance with the Englishman. Signing to Corinne, he drew to one side : they hit on some expedient promptly, for here was the girl facing Douglas again. " Won't you come upstairs with me ? "

" No, Corinne ; not even if Cardu is there too."

" You mean that you would feel safer if he were there than if we were alone ? "

"An ambiguous compliment, I admit; but it's true."

She broke into French, raised her voice and signified to Cardu that he must support her. "*Il m'a insultée,*" she cried dramatically, taking the whole room to witness; "*Il m'a honteusement insultée.*" She volunteered the information that *ce cochon d'Anglais* had treated her as if she were dirt, "*oui, à Londres, cet endroit infect de brouillards et de bêtas*": that he had struck her friend, *ce bon Cardu*, who nodded the most vigorous agreement. And now he had come here! "*J'ai bon caractère,*" she proclaimed to the onlookers, who, she saw, were enlisting rapidly on her side; as she finished the phrase, Brough hummed "*Je me laisse toujours faire*" and two unattached men laughed ("*Pas si bêtes, ces Anglais,*" grinned the one to the other). Corinne scowled at her slip, but continued to excite the waiters and the customers against Stevenson: they began to gather round the table threateningly. "Watch me and make a dash for it," whispered the cause of the trouble to his friends. He took a handful of one-franc pieces and five-franc notes from his pocket and threw them into the far corner of the room; this dispersed the group, which scattered to pick up the money. Cardu attempted to check the foremost of the three visitors, but he chose the wrong man as he realised when he recovered from the husky amateur boxer's punch on the point of his jaw. At the door, Douglas thrust a fifty-franc note in the "look-out's" hand. Once they were in the street they were safe: no fear of a hue and cry raised by a proprietor who avoided police-interference as much as possible. They returned to their lodgings, where, in Brough's room and over a bottle of his Madeira, the " hero " had to recount the English act of this little drama.

Apart from that incident he spent two uneventful but thoroughly enjoyable months in Paris. He worked at the Nationale and Arsenal libraries, read a little in the garden of the pension, and went about alone or with the Americans. He visited Versailles one Sunday to see the *grandes eaux*, and swore that he would never again risk it on a Sunday. He took a chance and tried several of the outer suburbs : his greatest find was Meudon, with its valley, its château, its observatory, its quiet and shady, almost rustic streets, and its pleasant woods. Often on a Sunday morning he would sit in the Luxembourg Gardens and watch the peculiar movement of Parisian life. Four successive Sunday afternoons were passed among the paintings and the statuary of the Louvre, where, contrary to the dictates of official opinion, he derived more pleasure from Ingres's *La Source* than from all the Titians and Rubens, Rembrandts and Ruysdaels, Velasquezes and Murillos. He was charmed by the general effect and separate pieces of the statuary-room at the Musée de Luxembourg, amused and interested by the orderly disorder of the Musée de Cluny ; agreeably surprised by the beauty of the windows and furniture of the Eglise de St. Etienne du Mont, with its bastard external architecture. He admired the comprehensive, masterly planning and ornament of the Arc de Triomphe, from the top of which he surveyed the avenues radiating like the spokes of a giant wheel ; climbed the Panthéon during a thunderstorm, obtained a wonderful view of Paris in the rain, with lightning-flashes dividing the city into lurid sections, and stayed to see the sun restoring the city to dazzling, clean-washed freshness ; attended a service at Notre-Dame, where afterwards he got a close view of the grotesque and fascinating gargoyles ; discovered the tranquil joy of sauntering along the bank of the Seine on a warm, moonlight night and (from across the river) gazing at different aspects of the cathedral. He experimented with the cafés and restaurants of the Boul' Mich' and its tributary streets, went once and once only to the Dôme and the Rotonde, and returned three or four times to several of the smaller restaurants on the Boulevard Montparnasse. Such districts exercised him far more than the magnificent but tourist-infested avenues and boulevards in the vicinity of the Opéra.

He went back to Oxford much refreshed. What remained of October behaved in the altogether delightful manner characteristic of the best Oxford autumns. If the vista up and down the river from Magdalen Bridge is enchanting in late spring, it is touchingly beautiful in early autumn ; if the sweep past Magdalen Tower to " the High " whips the blood to action in April, it will set both poets and hard-headed business-men a-dreaming in October ; if High Street, from Rose Lane to " the Turl " inspired Arnold in the rise, it just as surely enraptured Shelley in the fall of the year ; if the square of which the Camera is the impressive cynosure be lovely in the one, it is exquisite in the other ; if the streams call to youth on May Day, they chant a heart-twisting song to middle age, a quiet thanksgiving to eld when October arrives ; if Addison's Walk evokes a pæan of praise as one passes beneath a canopy of dark and delicate greens, it pervades with a subtle peace as one treads on the golden leaves ; if Christ Church meadow and Worcester garden and the swards of St. John's announce a world of beauty and a life of careless happiness when, arm-in-arm with a close friend, one strolls through them at the beginning of a summer term, they speak of a world where beauty fades but memory lives, of days of trouble with a sunset at the end, with God perhaps behind the veil, when one revisits them on the return to Oxford at the commencement of the academic year. Yet how much depends on circumstance! To the freshman, Oxford in October speaks of three happy years ; to the student who, when he takes his degree in July, looks on her for what is perchance the last time, Oxford brings a pain to his heart as he realises that he must leave the dear old place whose beauty he has never fully appreciated till now, and, furtively glancing about him lest anyone should see, he wipes away a tear : the only one that Oxford has caused him to shed.

Michaelmas and Hilary terms passed rapidly. In the summer, as he was walking near Iffley Lock, Douglas espied a couple lying amorously on the grass. He hastened on, his face troubled. Cardu and Corinne. What could they be doing here ? The most probable answer—it was, it happens the correct one—seemed to be that Cardu was with her as protector, while she was plying her profession in the town. Several nights later, as he returned home along Iffley road beneath the overhanging branches near the Red House, he shivered : he had the preposterous feeling that he was being shadowed. He turned round and saw a man lurch against the palings. "A drunk," he reflected, and hurried to his rooms.

The next night he was strolling with Brough, who had come to pay a visit to Oxford, along the lonely road that, past Iffley Turn, slopes rapidly on the way to Littlemore. It was late. Suddenly a shot rang out; Brough fell, with a bullet in his side. Douglas thought he heard a rustling in the grass on the bank above them. But he found nothing as he left the road and rushed up the slope. He returned to Brough, hailed a motor-car on its way into the town, and took the wounded man to the Infirmary. He went straight to the police and told them his suspicions. "We know the pair, I believe," remarked the inspector. By the last train leaving Oxford that night Cardu and Corinne attempted to escape; they were arrested as they were about to enter a carriage. It was Douglas they had intended to kill. Brough recovered; they were deported to France and sentenced to ten years' hard labour, and, after the long procedure of a French law-court, Douglas finished his career at Oxford without further excitement or mishap.

A CASE OF LUNACY

A CASE OF LUNACY

Gerald Harker was bored to extinction. As he walked restlessly up and down the sun-porch of his large house, effective from without and beautifully original from within, situated in the most pleasing part of the pleasing Manchester suburb of West Didsbury, he wondered what he could do to get a real kick out of life. Drunken bouts had not appealed to him even as a youth ; now that he was forty he disdained them. Adventurous in spirit, he had, both before and after the War (during which he served in the Air Force), gone with exploring parties into Central Asia, Central Africa and Central America, into the wilds of North-West Canada and the deserts of Australia, and, lastly, into New Guinea, where he had been speared in the hip : this misfortune, which, happening two years before the opening of this veracious story, left him rather lame, deprived him of the finest outlet for his high spirits.

On returning late in 1924 to Manchester, he had been content to rest awhile among his works of art, his curios, and his books, for next to adventurous travel and exploration, he loved the things of the mind and the senses. He had amused himself by sitting in the lounge of the Midland Hotel, looking romantic and lonely, receiving expressive glances from wealthy or beautiful women, and ignoring them to their intense annoyance. He had deliberately cultivated the acquaintance of a seemingly unapproachable, distinguished and pretty woman of his set (which was rich, intelligent and tolerably cultured), for he admired her wit and well-made figure : he took her by storm, discovered that she was very human, and shrank from consolidating so rapid a conquest ; not that he cast her off : he visited her every two or three weeks, and on those occasions, for which she lived, he found it easy—for she possessed both charm and lure—to make passionate love to her. But what was this in the life of a man who, having no need and little inclination to work, yet desired some engrossing activity or pursuit ?

He had been very disappointed at deriving only a temporary thrill from disguising himself as a workman and lounging, by day as well as by night, about the streets and public-houses of the two poorest districts in Manchester. For the sake of those who believe that there is nothing in the world to touch the slums of London, it may be recorded that Harker, who knew both cities, considered that the slums of Manchester were quite as tragic in their poverty and general wretchedness, though not quite so dangerous at night. For contrast, he had begun a course of research in Aztec customs by reading at the Rylands Library every afternoon (this was in April), but after a fortnight he abandoned that scholarly distraction, not because he wearied of it, but because he simply could not stay awake in that chemically-purified and scientifically-distributed atmosphere ; since he suspected that he snored (several of the numerous clergymen frequenting this architecturally-memorable building looked at him reprovingly and reproachfully when he resumed a more upright position) and since he objected to being heard to snore, he decided that this must cease. He had attended extra-mural and special lectures at the Victoria University and enjoyed the cultured, incisive and polished speaking of Stocks, the luminous, profound and witty address of his predecessor Alexander, the entertainingly informative lecture of Bragg, the very able, stimulating, and brilliantly-partial excursus of Charlton, the profound yet charming historianship of Powicke, the sparkling and alertly modern Classicism of Anderson : but while these lectures interested him vitally, they did not come often enough to protect him from boredom in the intervals. The theatres were insufficiently numerous to cater adequately for his wants, and the annual D'Oyley Carte season, one of the institutions of Manchester, was as an oasis ; the incidental, single plays of merit were few. Music came nearest to assuaging his restlessness : though a cosmopolitan, he supported Mancunians in their proud claim that theirs is the most musical city in Great Britain. Sometimes, if he happened to be in town on business, he would go to one of those excellent midday concerts. He belonged to several clubs, where his mordant wit made him enemies : he was not a natural clubman, for the club-bore fled him as if he were the avenging angel. In the old days he had often taken parties or partners to dance at the Midland and the Rivoli (as a dancing-floor, he preferred the latter), but now—well, Papua had been almost worth his disability. In the summer he had often run up to the hills in his two-seater and occasionally driven friends to the Lake District in his roadster. But it was not always summer, nor did he reckon to be a motor-fiend.

Perhaps the root of the trouble was that during the War he had lost two staunch friends, members of his own set : what they had delighted to do together, he found less amusing alone. Exploration had for five years prevented him from fully realising the gap that their deaths made in his life. He was thrown more than ever on his own resources by the spear-wound : just when those good friends would have helped the most, he was alone. Unmarried, he did not, for the present at least, think that he was likely to settle down. " Perhaps I should have married that girl I met at Altrincham," he thought ; " she might have saved me from this cursed boredom ! "

Long did Harker cast about in his search for some satisfying novelty. At last he hit on an idea that appealed to his cynicism, his intelligence, his recklessness. He would simulate madness : not stark-staring madness, but a pronounced eccentricity varied at pleasure with an amiable, entertaining lunacy. He took the precaution of assuring the maintenance of his sources and supplies of money, much of which was in consols. This, simply to content his flair for covering a retreat ; without prevision, without misgiving ; almost instinctively.

He began his campaign by hoaxing. One morning he strolled to the cinema near the Didsbury tram-terminus. On the pavement, he stood looking intently at the sky ; contrary to his usual practice, he wore spectacles. His gaze was so intent, his attitude so indicative of profound absorption as he leaned forward at a dangerous angle, that the local butcher-boy and the postman (pert, both of them, with the perkiness characteristic of the North of England) stopped and looked. Harker paid no attention to them : with exclamations of wonder and delight, he continued his rapt perusal of the apparently significant point of the heavens. " By Gad, he's got him! " he exclaimed.

" Who's got what, sir ? " queried the butcher-boy, unable to restrain his curiosity.

" Don't you see the small aeroplane lassoing that larger one ? " As he said this he turned round on the two spectators, laughed heartily in their faces, and walked off. " He's a rum 'un, all right," muttered the postman.

" What the 'ell's he up to ? " asked the boy indignantly.

Next day, Harker wrote a letter to *The Leeds Mercury*, for he feared that the congested columns of *The Manchester Guardian* would not house it. " Dear Sir," it ran, " It has lately fallen to my lot to witness an extraordinary incident, which some of your numerous intellectual readers may be able to explain. I have begged several of my friends for a solution of the problem in the acid of a mordant wit or by the aid of the precipitate of common-sense, which is oft akin to genius. Although they are notable chemists, they have failed to unravel this perplexed phenomenon. I believe that they are incapable of unravelling a phenomenon. But I have forgotten the golden dictum of Horace of Latin memory : *in medias res*, which being rendered into English meaneth : 'A good story needs no bush.' That reminds me, a bush played a small rôle in this drama of three ghosts enacted in the cemetery here. I was walking among the tombs (ever a pleasant custom of mine) several days ago, when, from behind a bush, started three ghosts, clothed, as a learned commentator of Shakespeare has it, in rags like the witches in Macbeth. At least, two were in rags ; the third man violated all the known habits of ghosts by appearing naked. I looked round hastily to see if there were any women near-by, for I would have you know, Sir, I am a great believer in the value of ignorance ; in fact, a friend of mine once told me that my own ignorance was worth millions. But pardon me, I wander from the subject. I spoke to them, and simultaneously the disciple of Adam, holding his arms aloft as his face shone forth so distinctly that it looked like an expressive death-mask at the fork of a living cross, raised his voice like to one crying in a graveyard. 'Woe to thee, thou cynic and borrower of insanity's cloak! I tell thee that ere the moon be again at its full, there shall be a wailing and gnashing of teeth in the house that is thy body. If these words be of things which are not, then wilt thou know it by the manner of our departure, for, if I lie, we shall depart even as human beings ; if I speak true, then . . .' His voice trailed off into an unearthly and creepy music as, with his comparatively respectable companions, he sank into the ground right against a worthy city-councillor's tombstone. The earth opened, disclosing a section of hell ; a jazz-band tortured the ears of those who had scoffed at the excellent chamber-music and stringed-quartettes of this city, an elysium of terrestrial music ; seated across from a philistine-critic, an especially malignant demon played a saxophone to the rustling of a note-book as a special reporter from *Punch* stood close at hand taking rapid notes, while near that devilish orchestra sat an

American student writing a Ph.D. thesis on the origin, development, influence, and results of nigger minstrelsy. I laughed aloud : the demons ceased from playing, the scene disappeared in smoke, but, before the obscurity became utter blackness, the naked ghost shook his fist and shouted : 'Woe unto thee, foul unbeliever!' The earth was healed of its satanic wound, no Arch-Fiend's scar remained. There stood I, gaping and astonied. A passing visitor approached me : 'You are not ill, I trust, sir!' I told him that I grieved for the loss of a dear friend. I hastened from out that cemetery. I wrote immediately to a noted novelist and spiritualist, but he confessed his inability to explain it ; and the same evening, I also sent a letter to Sir Roland Hodge, who opined that this might be a strange prefiguration of my fate after death ; I felt that this suggestion was lacking in tact. At a loss to account for the adventure, much too real to be purely psychic, I appeal, Sir, to the acknowledged good sense of your readers.

"I am, etc., Gerald Harker."

The hard-headed inhabitants of Leeds were silent. But some of his friends, both there and in Manchester, looked troubled. "What's happening to the fellow!" they exclaimed. An alienist doctor, an acquaintance, began to watch him closely when opportunity permitted. Moreover, the caprice of a week later made him a marked man.

He was due to deliver a lecture on *A Strange Journey*. It had been announced several months previously : his friends and acquaintances confidently expected that he would deal with the thrilling expedition up the Fly River in New Guinea. That was the subject on which he had intended to speak. But changing his mind, in accordance with his quest for eccentricity, he sent a copy to *Blackwood's*, where it appeared eight months later, and began to work up an address that would startle the brainy men from Withington and Fallowfield and upset the people from Didsbury. When the time came, he found a large audience awaiting him. With a peculiarly elusive smile, he advanced to the reading-desk.

" Mr. Chairman, ladies and gentlemen, on a night such as this, when the particular deity who regulates, makes mysterious, and damps the enthusiasm of our climate has done his best to throw a veil over the result, I feel that illumination would be peculiarly suitable [*laughter*], and, despite my well-known modesty, I say advisedly that my lecture contains much that is new, much that is original, much that is illuminating, even if the light is of a somewhat disturbing kind : of a variety that some of you may be tempted to describe as Coleridgean. Not the less interesting on that account, I trust. Well, immediately after I had finished writing out the lecture which I had intended to deliver, with amplifications, to you here, an awesome figure arose at my elbow. With a disarming colloquialism, however, he reassured me as he said : ' No cause to be frightened. I am here to ask you if you would care to have the material for a much more exciting lecture than that. Not that it is in the least dull : I've heard much less justifiable papers read at the R.G.S.' He beckoned me to follow, and, with the intrepidity that *The Daily Mail* has been so rash as to declare a characteristic of all my poor exploits, I walked out of my study and into the night. A car rushed us away at a sickening speed. We stopped on a lonely country road, near the crest of a slope. My guide opened a concealed door on the bank. On entering, I saw that I was in a dimly-lit corridor, at the end of which was a huge cavern. The audience was picturesque and motley, consisting as it did of men and women of all countries and periods. 'All these persons,' said Beaumarchais (for it was he), 'have at some time or other felt an *ennui* no less oppressive than yours. When I made them acquainted with your condition—for you must know that I am a kind of modern Mercury—they unanimously decided to invite you to come here that you might be initiated into this distinguished society and thus enjoy the privileges that it confers.' The ceremony was performed by Napoleon, who, it seems, was the victim of an intolerable *ennui* during the earlier part of the wars so gratifyingly named after him, when he was winning victory after victory.

The privilege most valued was that which allowed a new member to command any and every old one to show him, on a cinema screen, the most thrilling, the most wonderful, or the most delightful day in his life. I called first on Napoleon to display the most wonderful of his days : he turned a handle of what looked like a hurdy-gurdy ; all one end of the cavern became a screen ; his coronation as Emperor was shown. Evidently Napoleon considered that this pageant set a seal on his prestige and served to indicate and stress the tremendous actual power that lay behind the glitter and the pomp. Two days after (I was magnificently lodged, I ate and slept well, and had all the while a curiously satisfying sense of elation), I invited Julius Cæsar to let me see the most thrilling day in his variegated career : I watched him overcoming Cicero in a long and heated debate ; his delight in his concise, telling, polished sentences and dagger-like phrases was infectious, although I could not help being a little sorry for his opponent. 'So this,' I asked him later, 'was the day that you consider the most thrilling.'

'Without any doubt,' he replied enthusiastically ; 'my military exploits were the result of a national tradition sharpened to individuality and irresistibility by my unconscious genius and by compulsory service in the army. To gain that victory over Cicero, I had studied and striven for years, I had practised in the hills or among my friends, and tried my strength with many an unworthy opponent till I should possess confidence.'

This society was able not only to show the various scenes but to reproduce the accompanying words exactly as they had been spoken : the movietone, as they call the process, will, in a year or two, be given to mortals, for Beaumarchais finds his work becoming too strenuous and the membership list will soon be full. The commands of Napoleon, the arguments of Cæsar were as convincing to me as they must presumably have been in the bygone years. The latter's *journée* caused me to think of Marc Antony, whom, for the sake of variety, I summoned to present the most delightful day in his—if so distinguished an audience will pardon me the use of slang (he bowed with genial and captivating courtesy)—in his somewhat hectic life. 'In fact, sir,' I said gravely, 'I claim the second privilege.' This states that once in the series of pictures, the member may name the day.

'In other words, Sir, I ask you to show the happiest of your days or nights with Cleopatra. Now Marc Antony does not agree with those who would have no talk of love, who deny that passion can be an integral part—nay, the only adequate physical manifestation—of love, who believe that there should be no instruction in passion. To such intellectual, sensible persons as we are, his opinions are ridiculous : he actually held that, as one derives more pleasure from playing a game well than from playing it badly, clumsily and unintelligently, so in sexual relations [*several of the audience blushed, many stirred uneasily*] one should know how to extract the most delight from the various caresses ; and, in answer to the objections of those who think that such knowledge and such aims would destroy or lessen the emotional ecstasy, he said that the knowledge and the aims, soon becoming habitual, would thus exact no thought and therefore would not impair the ecstasy in the least. Such nonsense is not for us, who keep to the right line of inexpert tradition and unimaginative practice : for an Englishman to give his attention to the development and enrichment of sexual pleasure,—however sincere, however far-seeing, however correct in his theories he may be,—is to brand him as either morbid or filthy-minded or satyriatic : for him to write about such things is to convict him of an unpardonable lack of reticence, of forsaking Saxon reserve and manliness for Latin shamelessness and effeminacy. Marc Antony amplified these points, but, as I perceive that some of you suspect that I think with him thereon, I shall continue my narrative. Can I, however, do this? For the Roman that reckoned the world well lost for a mistress whose infinite variety custom could not stale, revealed his most wondrous night of love. The knowledge I gained from that picture would enable me, if so I wished, to become a more formidable lover than Don Juan or Casanova. But such a career is not for me [' *No!*' *said the alienist doctor to himself*] : I am less ambitious. To prove to you the nature of the representation, Marc Antony insisted that it should be *in camera* ; in other words, that a curtain should be so drawn across the hall that a small space remained for Antony and myself, while the rest of the assembly played cards, gossiped, read and drank behind it. 'Why this secrecy ? ' I whispered to the Roman.

' It would send Cæsar mad, for though he pretends that his affair with Cleopatra was merely a casual amour, he had a passion for her. Moreover, some of the company, despite their being great statesmen or generals, scientists or scholars, poets or dramatists, with perhaps a reputation for being a little—shall we say, puritanical—in their habits, were no better than a libertine *bon viveur* when they found themselves alone with a pretty girl or an alluring woman : the sight of our caresses might induce lewd thoughts, and then we would have these men and the few women admitted to the society conducting an orgy in the manner of Imperial Rome at its worst. Unedifying, my friend. Whereas, what you are about to see . . . ' The tone of his voice implied the opinion that this would result in valuably instructive and even edifying knowledge. The pen of Gautier might possibly have been equal to the task of conveying an adequate impression of that night, when Cleopatra was a marvel of various sensuality and Antony a signal reproach to us effete men [*several learned persons looked as if they indignantly repudiated the animadversion*]. I, naturally, must content myself with repeating that Gautier *might* have succeeded where I would fail. Lest you think that I am describing a dream, I tell you frankly that every detail of that epic of love is printed on my mind and that I may perhaps issue, for private circulation, an account of it ; anyone desirous of obtaining a copy should write to me at my private address ; I guarantee complete secrecy. Certain marriages that are now cruel mockeries, certain women whose affection for their husbands is as ignorant as it is cold, certain men who are little more effective than eunuchs,—these might be respectively rectified, rendered lovingly ingenious, and made a credit to their sex as well as a joy to their wives. I would be prepared to give private——"

He was about to say "advice," but the audience thought that he intended to say "demonstrations." Loud murmurs were heard from every part of the hall; the women were uncomfortably agog; the men felt that the last two statements had far exceeded the bounds of eccentricity, good form, and ordinary decency. The audience rose as one man and, throwing wrathful and scornful glances over their shoulders, marched out. What a scandal! they called a meeting and discussed what should be done. They would have preferred to hush up the affair so far as the public was concerned and to deal with Harker privately : they were in doubt as to whether he were merely pulling their leg (" In that case he has gone too far ; a joke is a joke, dammit," bellowed Colonel Fireribs), whether he were mad (" That means a lunatic asylum for him," said the doctor judicially), whether he were suffering from a hallucination ("Even then," asserted the doctor, "he must be watched"), or whether, having a general grudge, he wished to insult his audience *en masse* ("It would be difficult for us all to obtain damages," observed a little man of much sense). After further discussion, they agreed that it was almost certainly either a hoax or madness. The doctor's opinion, ably and eloquently expressed, carried the day. It was decided to bring a charge of lunacy, conducted by the alienist and corroborated by certain members of the audience.

Meanwhile, Harker, thinking that his auditors had departed in a wrath that would cool before the sun set next day, slipped into his car and returned home in high spirits at the success of his lecture. "Really," he spluttered, "they stood a lot more than I'd have tolerated in their place." He slept better than he had done for two years, awoke to find the sun reproaching him for a slugabed, and leapt out as if he had no "game" leg. "Great to be alive!" he thought; "I'll run down to London for a week."

When he returned, the charge was ready. Not only the eccentricities that we have recorded but many slighter, though not less suspicious, details were adduced. The doctor had collected the evidence with skill and cunning. He believed that Harker was going, was perhaps already, mad; he did not know, nor was he wholly convinced. But he did not wish to know and he did not feel the necessity to be convinced, for this was a chance thrown at him by his enemy, who was delivering himself into his hands more completely than Charles Williams had dreamt it would be possible for him to do. Dr. Williams hated him with a consuming, malignant, perfectly-concealed hate : Harker considered him one of the most charming and interesting of his acquaintances. But while the explorer was in southern seas that last time, the doctor had fallen in love with a certain woman ; he thought he was sure to win her and thus at one blow obtain a bride and a fortune, the one honourably desired, the other less honourably coveted ; Harker returned, conquered the lady, did not marry her, but, as we have seen, continued at intervals to visit her ; not being one of those women who are " caught on the rebound," she gave Williams no encouragement.

Had Gerald Harker remained that week in Manchester, he would have guessed that trouble was brewing : probably he would have gone to live on a plantation that he owned high up on the Ceylonese hills, where the temperature was tolerable, where tropical flowers, accumulated and cultivated in an irregular circle around the building, caused the bungalow to resemble a squat and attractive lighthouse in a sea of blooms, and where he would find congenial friends among his English neighbours ; or else have promptly confuted the rumours, laughingly acknowledged the hoaxes and caprices, and behaved convincingly in his normally alert, sane, intelligent manner. The charge was brought against him immediately he returned. At first he could not believe that this was anything but a practical joke (" Serve me right! " he exclaimed) made to pay him out for his own. When he saw that the charge was serious, he raged with fear, indignation and disgust. When he regained his nerve, it occurred to him that he might as well " carry on." At the inquiry, therefore, he refused to say anything to disprove the charge and even delivered himself of some wildly extravagant speeches. That clinched the matter.

In due course he became an inmate of the impressive local lunatic asylum. The affair provided the newspapers with badly-needed " copy " : it was a lean time. He had verified and ensured the safety of his money ; on one score, then, he was at peace. For several months he continued to simulate lunacy, but, as you may know, it is very hard to bring off hoaxes in an asylum, the other inmates being too engrossed with themselves to attend, the staff being rightly suspicious ; he was, therefore, confined to verbal aberrations. These were over the heads of the warders. The doctors, however, esteemed him no less remarkable than mad : "A man whose sweetness has been destroyed by an excess of light," said one of them. Dr. Callan was puzzled by Harker, whom he could not convict of sanity, but who seemed at times to have one leg in the land of the sane. The patient read widely : at first he had difficulty in obtaining the books he wanted, but he soon got his own way, for not only was he able and ready to pay, but, if a book were not forthcoming, he made trouble : on these refusals he became violent and noisy. Callan was particularly struck by certain features in this case : there was a strange desultoriness in Harker's deviations from the straight path ; he had no special mania, the eccentricities and extravagances covering a wide field ; he rarely buttonholed visitors ; he was never mad when medical students appeared ; and he discerned all specialists. One day a great authority on lunacy arrived at the asylum ; Dr. Callan, delegated to show him over the building, passed him Harker's chart ; "An unusually difficult case ; I sometimes think that we ought to discharge him ; in fact I would be glad if you could have a look at him. Your word would go." The subject of the conversation caught the last sentence, grasped its significance, and decided that he did not wish to leave yet awhile. The truth was that he had become so intrigued by what he saw around him, and derived such a zest from keeping up his own appearances while he was making a close study of the lunatics, that he determined to stay until he had a good general knowledge of the signs and tendencies of lunacy and the solution of several knotty points. As the " very famous man " approached, Harker assumed a cynical grin and sneered : " Pot-Calling-the-Kettle-Black, canst thou minister to a mind diseased ? " He then laughed raucously and put out his tongue at the specialist, who, slightly annoyed, said sharply : " Is *your* mind diseased ? " Doctors don't make a habit of asking that question, but then very rarely does a madman assert or admit his madness. Harker perceived what lay back of the question, smiled fatuously, and replied : " Sir Edmund . . ." The others started. " How do you know my name ? " he asked. "A few minutes ago I heard you saying pompously to my dear and unfortunate friend, Dr. Callan, that ' Sir Edmund Dolittle never makes a mistake.' I wish to have only this little to do with you, sir : to state that a man so crassly and naïvely persuaded of his infallibility as you, should be standing in my place, while Dr. Callan, whose brilliant essay on incipient insanity I read before the infuriating blackness enveloped me as with a cloak of suffocating stupidity, should be given your job. Sir Polichinelle, Harlequin bids you adieu! " Upon which, he ran out of the room laughing with genial scorn and, at the exit, made an exaggeratedly low bow. Callan felt that the situation called for tact : " One of his worst days." An unnecessarily severe note was entered by Dolittle on the offender's chart ; " I had a pretty thin time of it," confided Callan to a fellow-doctor. Great pals, these two : they had roughed it in sister battalions in Salonika. Callan described Harker and his case in detail. They decided that something was amiss, the more so as they knew of a shady incident in Williams's undergraduate days (they had not divulged it, for it might have brought some slight discredit on the good name of the medical school) and disliked him : in short, they regarded with suspicion his share in Harker's confinement.

Callan began to watch his patient more closely than ever, but, for a year longer, Harker continued to give a convincing display of mental derangement. So soon as he had completed his private investigations, he said to Callan : " Might I speak to you privately, Doctor ? " The result of the long conversation was that Harker proved his sanity. He went before the next board. Immediately he was discharged, he betook himself to the house of Williams, whom he soundly thrashed and even more thoroughly shamed. His liberation was a local nine days' wonder, but his acquaintances could not quite forgive him for having made such fools of them ; nor, of course, was he likely to go out of his way to repair the rift. He sold up his home and sailed for that bungalow perched on a pleasantly beautiful hill in Ceylon's finest tea-growing district. There he lives a comfortable, cheery life, is the most popular diner-out in the whole of the island, enjoys an enviable reputation as an amateur alienist, and draws disgustingly large royalties from his book entitled : *Eighteen Months in a Manchester Mad-House.*

CHARMIAN WARRINGTON

CHARMIAN WARRINGTON

Miss Charmian Warrington embarked at Southampton. No one knew her ; it was not likely that they should. As a child she had left England for New York, and on her return to London at the end of November, 1926, she was so disgusted with the English winter that after a week of it she went to Paris for two months. She had money, self-respect, a vivid interest in art and literature ; she was at home in most circles ; restrained in manner, graceful in movement, she usually gave the impression of being reserved—so in fact she was, with strangers and acquaintances, and she made few friends. The quietness and the reserve were largely the result of two widely-divergent characteristics : she had an original, independent mind and a capacity for passionate companionship so thoroughly recognised by her that she knew its potentialities and proudly respected its value. She did not wish to waste herself on a frivolous society nor to squander herself on a man that might be unworthy : as her standards were exceedingly high, she was usually regarded by men as distant and cold.

Paris charmed her, but as she could afford to indulge a caprice she did not hesitate to book a passage to Melbourne when she heard that her best girl friend had gone to live there. She obtained an airy outside berth on a P. & O. steamer leaving England in the middle of February. The weather, as far as Gibraltar, was raw and wet, but the Bay of Biscay failed to live up to its somewhat daunting reputation—a defection of which she approved. The gaunt and impressive Portuguese coast, however, appealed to her love of nature untrammelled. Yet she anticipated with pleasure the ball announced to take place on the eve of the ship's arrival in Gibraltar. In the late afternoon, smartly dressed in a tweed tailor-made, she strolled on the promenade deck, enjoying the tang of the moisture-laden air and wondering in which frock she would look her best; with a due regard for her health, she decided that she would wear a heavy silk dress that promised warmth and charm, for its close-fitting cut displayed to advantage her admirable figure, a rare blending of Diana's and of Juno's, with its grace and faintly voluptuous attractiveness. Pausing a moment, she turned (she could not have said why) to glance at a man who sat reading; she knew that book and, while somewhat repelled by its cynical eroticism, had enjoyed its brilliant wit. From the expression on his face, it seemed that he was re-acting in a similar fashion to *Antic Hay*. "Neither rake nor sybarite, neither sophisticate nor simpleton," she thought. "Perhaps thirty-five; looks as if he had roughed it a bit, though not wholly by choice. Intelligent too." Under her unconsciously penetrating gaze, he glanced up at the pleasing stranger, held her eyes a moment, and, without smiling or showing the least interest, returned to Aldous Huxley. She coloured ever so little and was annoyed at doing so; she resumed her walk, but on the other side of the ship. Wondering vaguely if he danced, she went below to her cabin to dress for dinner, which was at seven o'clock. Always fastidious, she devoted rather more time than usual to her toilet, appeared to be dissatisfied with her face (although its *brune* beauty would have been prized by most women), and spent forty minutes in arranging her dark-brown hair : one indication of her individuality was that she wore it long, without sentimentalising about " woman's crowning glory " or resenting the well-meaning persuasions of those girls who, with perhaps a trace of envy, would have her cut it short, to bob, to shingle or to bingle, to adopt the Eton or any other crop. Nor did she shave her eyebrows, which in their natural state accorded well with dark, sombrous but by no means sombre eyes.

At dinner she received a shock when the chair beside her, previously vacant, was occupied by the reader of *Antic Hay*. The explanation was simple. Wilfrid Cunningham, when he came aboard, was suffering from a slight relapse of malaria. After a day in bed, he went on deck every morning and afternoon for a couple of hours, but he continued to eat in his cabin. The afternoon Charmian first saw him, he had recovered, although, not particularly hungry, he absented himself from lunch. He did not speak to her for some time except to pass the cruet. But life aboard ship is a sociable affair, and when, in reply to the enquiry of an old colonel sitting opposite, he mentioned why he had not been seen at table, she turned and asked gently : " You are quite well now ? "

" Oh, nothing wonderful! but not too bad, thank you." Otherwise the conversation remained general.

The ball (though its informality hardly justified the name) commenced at a quarter to nine, the ship's

" orchestra," consisting of three, supplying the music. Charmian did not dance the first number, a one-step. For the next, a fox-trot, the colonel wondered if he might have the honour. Yes, he might. It was perhaps more appreciated by him than by her, though she found his well-worn stories amusing. As the opening bars of the third dance floated out on the waves (luckily the night was calm), Wilfrid Cunningham strolled along. " Might I have the pleasure of this waltz ? " They danced. Malaria had not affected his step, which was smooth, rhythmic, almost perfect. They spoke little, but they agreed as if they had long been partners. " You like music ? " he asked.

" Why music ? "

" Because no one could dance so exquisitely without loving music : you dance with, not merely to, the tune."

" By the same token you must be passionately fond of it."

"That is quite true," he replied ; "but I don't deserve the compliment you have passed on my dancing. If I'm dancing well, the merit is yours." Then after a pause : "*I* wonder would you play to me some day."

" Who said I could play ? " she retorted.

" No one, but I'm pretty sure that you do."

" Well, perhaps I shall."

Several days later, when the social hall was almost empty, she was sitting near the piano. Cunningham came up to her. " That promise," he said, with a glance at the piano.

" Does *perhaps* constitute a promise ? What would you like me to play ? "

"Anything that it would give you pleasure to play."

She sat down at the piano, and, with profound feeling, rendered a piece from a Brahms' *opus*. Her technique, though excellent, was not such as would have gained her a prize at the Conservatoire de Paris, but the understanding, the emotion, the sympathy displayed in this, as in the two pieces (a Beethoven and a Debussy) that followed, made the music lovely no less to ordinary human beings than to the *cognoscenti*. She gave herself wholly to the playing; when she finished, she sat motionless awhile. Cunningham rose, went to the piano, and said: "Thank you." No fulsome compliments, no exaggerated praise: the tone expressed enough approval and delight to satisfy Charmian, who set no fictitious value on speech. After a moment of silence, he suggested that they might take a turn on deck together.

This, however, was after Gibraltar, where Charmian went ashore, but found nothing particularly interesting in the dusty streets, with their very mixed architecture; they can, in summer, be like ovens. From the open sea or from the "harbour," Gibraltar is one of the most imposing and majestic of sights, rendered all the more significant that, apart from the massiveness of the rock, its strength is veiled: at no point from the sea can one distinguish the guns, hidden as they are in galleries and run out as need demands, and no one but soldiers and trusted officials are allowed anywhere near them. Bare, upright and high, Gibraltar carries its menace with dignity, its power disguised. *The Peninsula of the Iron Glove*, was the description she gave to Cunningham. "Why did you not go ashore ?" she enquired, as she mounted the gangway to find him leaning over the side.

"Well, I felt a little tired after the dancing last night. But I know Gib. quite well. Was here for a month in 1917."

"As one of the garrison ?"

"No ; I was in the Intelligence Department and moved round a good deal in the Mediterranean, like the Johnny in one of Mason's books."

She nodded : "Martin something-or-other. But you must have been rather young at the time for such dangerous and—and——"

"Shall we say 'mature' work ?"

"Yes, that's the word."

"Well, I suppose I was, for soon after I left Marlborough I went out East, but, catching malaria, I tranferred my activities to Mediterranean waters, where I still was on the outbreak of war. I had been there about three years ; knew every port of any size and many islands with hardly a right to a name. My knowledge was considered useful by the Intelligence crowd, to one of whom my father gave me an introduction when he heard that I intended to enlist. Although I wished at first to go into the infantry or—though I knew nothing about aeroplanes—into the air-force, 'the head serang of the intelligentsia' (as one of my pals called him) persuaded me to join his lot."

"You were not a mere spy, were you ?"

"Do I look as I might have been ?"

"No, I'm sorry," she exclaimed ; "you were probably less of an agent than of a kind of gentleman adventurer."

"Most discerning of you. But, you may believe me, it wasn't all beer and skittles, for although I was never in hostile territory, I was on several occasions the only Britisher in small Greek and Spanish ports, cess-pits for the scum of the earth, hot-beds for enemy spies. Got this one night." He showed her the scar on his third finger, which, as she had noticed, he had difficulty in bending.

"Were you resting when you were at Gibraltar?"

"Nominally. That was part of the 'blind.' I ran to earth a slippery Spanish agent in German employ. No, he made a blunder: I was lucky enough to be present (though I'll admit that I was intentionally present) at the time. One of those little details that mean nothing to the uninitiated, everything to the man engaged on the same or similar work. A little expert knowledge often spares one the necessity of being a Sherlock Holmes: that, you know, is why Scotland Yard sometimes calls on chemists—no, not pharmaceutists—to assist it. They might more often enlist the aid of chemists and they might also use the brains of professional men, of authorities in various fields. But that's their look-out."

"You said that you were three years in the Mediterranean. Would it be impertinent . . . ?"

"Not at all, Miss Warrington. I'm not a rich man, but I have enough to render work, in the ordinary sense, unnecessary. At Marlborough, I was frightfully keen on Geography, even at the stage at which one usually passes to other subjects. The Mediterranean had always rather attracted me. I had decided to make a study of the ports, from the Levant to Gibraltar. Had a large and practically unsubmersible motor-boat, strong and fast; a topping sea-craft she was too. In the middle of summer I ran from Plymouth to this old rock; you can bet I ascertained what the Bay of Biscay would probably be like before I made that run."

"I suppose you had someone with you?"

"Yes, a Plymouth man. What he didn't know about the sea wouldn't fill a page in a pocket-diary. Very silent. But good-tempered and a real handy-man. He stayed with me all the time, even during the war, though I had a little difficulty in wangling that."

"But you surely weren't at it—I mean before the war—all the time!"

"No, I laid off from the beginning of December until the end of March; otherwise, I was in the Mediterranean for four months in the first calendar year (1912), eight months on end during the next, and four months in 1914. The chief ports occupied, by comparison, the most of my time, but I gave much attention to the others; and in 1913 and '14 I began also to examine the uninhabited or sparsely-inhabited bays and inlets. The latter pursuit soon came to fascinate me so much that I devoted to it much more time than I did to the study of the ports. As you might guess, my knowledge of the less-known regions was regarded as invaluable by the Intelligence people."

Charmian wished to hear more of his pre-war excursions. She was a good listener; her questions were sensible and sometimes extraordinarily shrewd, with the shrewdness that derives not from wide experience or cunning but from a searching imagination. Cunningham, who very rarely spoke of his life in the

Mediterranean, let himself go because he felt that she was genuinely interested. He talked well, with a felicitous phrase ever and anon illuminating the objective and realist manner of his narrative; he was evidently observant of men as well as of places, with a gift of rapid characterisation; and he had a sense of humour, which showed in his lively accounts of how, when he was new to his hobby, he was often cheated in the Levant and the Ægean. When she asked about the beauty of the setting sun's coronation of Stromboli, of the Golden Horn, of Naples from the bay, and the like, he replied:

"But you seem to have been here before."

"No; I've read a little, that's all. Have always been interested in the Inland Sea, which was good enough for the old Greeks and Romans."

Shyly, he told of those three sights and others; his description remained picturesque and to some extent precise and objective, but something of idealism and poetry informed the words, while now and then came a phrase that might have fitted into a lyric. "Despite his wanderings," she reflected, "he has remained very English in his unwillingness to be thought poetical. If one asked him if he wrote verses, he would blush to the roots of his hair." Then she darted at him: "Do you write poetry?"

He looked very confused and disconcerted: "Not so as you'd notice," he answered.

"I'm like you," she responded immediately, "I write very little, and I'd hate anyone to know of it."

"Well, I know of it."

"Yes, but you are not a stranger."

He gazed a moment full in her eyes; his hand

brushed hers. She showed neither annoyance nor pleasure, but said, with the merest flutter in her voice, "I must get a book out of the library before it closes."

On the journey to Gibraltar to Marseilles they slowly improved the acquaintance: or rather, the bond had, from the outset, been of such stuff as friendship and dreams are made of. The man knew that he was falling in love, for, when he was twenty-one, he had been jilted. But this, he realised, was different. "I'm for it," he muttered with a humorous smile. She had not gone so far, but she divined that, circumstances aiding, the friendship might easily become something else. Aged twenty-eight, she had, soon after she came of age, fallen in love with a French artist in New York. Their relations were those of lover and mistress. Within a few months he had died of pneumonia, and, though much courted, she had not coquetted in the least degree till now, when the coquetry was not superficial, but instinctive.

"Do you know Marseilles, Miss Warrington?"

"No; but that's the Château d'If, isn't it! Jolly story, *Le Comte de Monte-Cristo*. I read it in an English translation and abominably small print, when I was ten, and I read it for the fourth time when I was twenty-one."

"Once more than I have done. But may I show you the sights of Marseilles? There's an interesting church to which one ascends by a funicular, part of the old town is worth seeing, and I'd like to take you for a run along the sea-shore to the Corniche."

"That's very kind of you, but perhaps you have some friends here that you'd like to see."

" I have friends here, but I would rather act cicerone to my new friend, if you will permit me to think of you as such ? "

" Thought is free," she replied, " and, since we're so confidential " (a quick smile lit her face to sunny loveliness), " I may say that I consider you as a friend."

" Like that, you are beautiful," he exclaimed impulsively as he watched her ; and then he blushed.

A soft light shone an instant in her eyes, but she was careful to hide it from him. " Hadn't we better be going ? " she queried steadily, with her voice clear and comradely.

They visited the places he had mentioned and afterwards enjoyed tea at a small café. Throughout, he was helpful, restrained, yet amusing. She liked him the more for his apparent forgetfulness of the awkward moment that, four hours before, had shown her that he loved her. " I think that I should give you a badge or a certificate to prove how grateful I am for so pleasant a jaunt."

For three days she saw him rather less than before. Perhaps he was testing the strength of his regard for her. At meals, however, he was attentive and agreeable ; he joined in the general conversation and might even be said to have shone in it. Those three days served him better than he knew, for Charmian had time to take stock of her feelings.

" Yes, I love him," she said to herself the third night, as she looked into the mirror.

The next day, immediately before they went in to breakfast, she found him on deck. " Have I offended you ? " she asked.

"Oh, no! what made you think that?"

"Nothing. Only, I wondered. You seemed to be avoiding me."

"Perhaps I was. The reason, however, was quite different from the one you have suggested."

Nothing more was said, but that was the turning point.

On arriving at Port Said in the morning, Cunningham proposed that, as they had four hours clear before lunch, they should visit the principal mosque, go through and around the town in a gharry, and take coffee at the chief hotel ("There's a rather nice lounge," he added). As they were driving on the outskirts, he gently took her hand, held it awhile and thrilled as she almost imperceptibly (yet not quite imperceptibly—that was the important distinction!) returned the pressure; for a moment he clasped her hand warmly between both of his before releasing it. When, on reaching the mosque, they had perforce to exchange their shoes for the flat slippers that for some reason or other (perhaps because they are made of vegetable, not animal, matter; perhaps also because they are not contaminated by commerce with the world outside) do not offend against the holiness and sacredness of the edifice, whereas the visitor's shoes would desecrate its sanctity, Cunningham unintentionally glimpsed a very attractive foot, neat and shapely in its silk. Charmian was much less interested in the city intrinsically than in its significance as the half-way house between East and West—the natives having all the white man's vices, none of his virtues; the unofficial population consisting mainly of the worst specimen of natives and the white scum of the earth ; the façade, as it were, being clean and white as one views the buildings from the harbour, whereas the city itself, apart from perhaps four streets, drowns the good, pure and beautiful in the thoroughly bad, filthy and ugly. Even now, the greater part of Port Said is unsafe to walk through by night ; even now, if one has enemies in this port, it is a far, far better thing to keep to the beaten path than to deviate therefrom by even one alley-way ; as it has always been, so is it now, an extensively and foully diseased city of thieves, swindlers, and cut-throats, with an official population (the best of the shopkeepers and the like may be added) sharply separated ; if the white man does not remember his caste and his colour, he is dragged into an inextricable vortex of intrigue, shame and vice. As Cunningham, who knew his Port Said well, could have told her, the observant traveller that stays there for more than the usual half-day sees faces that puzzle. Somebody dressed in native clothes slouches by, yet the features are European ; there are men professing the Mohammedan faith who once were Roman Catholics ; several years ago, there followed the calling of guide, one who, rather better clad than most guides, spoke Arabic perfectly, but whose tanned and bearded face, if scrutinised closely, was seen to be that of an English aristocrat. One would like to investigate the native quarters, the wharfside, perhaps also the most cosmopolitan of the lower strata, for the research and documentation would yield startling, illuminating, all-engrossing results, but the task would be extremely difficult, certainly endangering one's life and possibly hazarding one's soul. If, however, one spoke Arabic and some useful dialect to perfection, if one were strong of health and sinew, if one were alert, courageous, prudent, and if one had several reserves of money (the last requisite is probably the most important), the undertaking would be feasible, but, for it to be thoroughly profitable, one would have to live thus for several years. Cunningham dwelt on this idea as he sat with Charmian at a corner table overlooking the bustle of one of the two most important streets, where native vendors, tourists, and officials mingled to form a picturesque scene. " I agree with you that it would be a wonderful experience, that is if one survived to be able to call it an experience," she said ; " nevertheless, I hope you're not considering the project seriously."

" I was," he replied, with a slight emphasis on the past, " but now I think that perhaps there are pursuits better worth while."

At two in the afternoon the ship moved from her moorings. The northern end of the Suez Canal is less interesting than the southern, but as they stayed on deck till midnight, Charmian saw most of it and had little cause for regret as she listened to Cunningham's description of the southern entrance as one comes into it at night, with Port Suez on the left, the electric lamps illuminating the shore, the palm-trees gracefully setting-off the bungalows behind them, the ripple and gleam of the water as the vessel, with scarcely a sound and hardly a noticeable movement save that of progress, glided along. The salt lakes engage one's attention, more especially if there are numerous native boats ; the remains of trenches remind one how important it once was to prevent the enemy reaching the canal; at intervals one passed the stations, which, housing the staff responsible for its upkeep, provided a relief of green to the parched sands on both sides; a native occasionally ambled by on a camel. What Charmian didn't see, was described in detail to her by her companion. Many others remained late on deck, but once, as they stood on the fore-part of the promenade, watching the long line of the Canal fleeing ever before them, they found themselves alone as they rested their elbows on the rail. His further hand closed over hers, his arm, slipping round her, drew her close, and thus they stayed until footsteps approached and they regained a more strictly conventional position. Nothing had been said, but there was no need: she had yielded to his clasp. The intruders passing into the obscurity, he put an arm about her again, with the other brought her facing him, and, after a mutually searching, equally troubled look, they kissed as though each meant the other to understand that, by this act, they became lovers; body clung to body; her breasts were crushed against him as he folded her passionately close, her arms going round his neck. "Charmian, you are wonderful," he breathed.

"And you, Wilfrid, you're—but I won't tell you. Not now at least."

"How I want you!" he murmured with slow intensity and with a tormenting pain vibrating in his voice.

"Don't! oh, don't!" She spoke quietly, but her words were charged with longing. Then: "Good-night, my dear," she said; "I must go now."

They moved off together. Just before they came

into the wide open part of the deck, he stopped. "Before you go," he whispered, as he kissed her gently on the forehead; she pressed his hand a moment. At the staircase where they parted, she to descend, he to stay a few minutes on deck, they exchanged a long expressive look and, without a word, went their ways.

The Red Sea, decidedly less hot at the end of February than during the months of June, July and August, is none the less "trying" whatever the season. The men change into flannels, the women begin to leave things off; the dancing so frequent in the Mediterranean loses its zest. Charmian and Wilfrid strolled or sat about together. The strength of their mutual regard may be gauged from the fact that she decided to disembark at Aden, take a boat to Bombay, go thence to Colombo, and there catch the next P. and O. liner for Australia simply because he was visiting Bombay and begged her to accompany him; while he, instead of stopping at that port for a month as he had originally intended, arranged to travel down to Colombo with her and proceed to Melbourne in the same ship.

At Aden they sent their luggage by tender across to the other vessel, while they chartered a motor-boat to run them into that sun-baked township nestling on the narrow shore at the foot of the barren ridge. They motored out to visit the cisterns but were not persuaded to visit those "mermaids" which gullible travellers still pay to see. More wisely they sat for some time on the verandah of the only really decent hotel and sipped that favourite drink of the tropics, gin and ginger-beer.

The trip from Aden to Bombay is short, but Charmian did not greatly enjoy it, for she knew that "people were talking." At Bombay, they stayed at different hotels, but met in order to shop in the native quarter, to look at several magnificent mosques, to drive along the well-laid roads of Malabar Hill, where the residences, set amid trees and sometimes built around a fountain-court, make one wishful to live in the East. The higher English officials and the big merchants, whether European or Parsee, certainly understand the art of enjoying the clear skies and rainless days; yet their homes are almost equally pleasant during the rainy season. Bombay is, in most ways, the finest city in India: magnificent, delicate, elaborate Oriental architecture; minarets rising from clumps of dark-green foliage; bazaars insolent and barbaric in their riotous variety of colour; excellent European shops (such as the "Army and Navy") for European needs; cool, fascinating arcades; swarming natives. There is less disaffection, fewer agitators here than in most of the large Indian cities: Charmian and Wilfrid, in a non-political way, were alive to such problems of government.* In their discussion of the quandary of

* They noticed that the disaffection was spread considerably by, the agitators recruited largely from, those numerous Indian students who travel to England (the Universities of Oxford, Cambridge and London are their goal) to advance their knowledge, and then, having been kindly treated and unselfishly aided, return to India to incite the ignorant natives against British rule. Not that all Indian students do this: some are inspired with a profound love of learning and ask for nothing more than to devote their lives to its cultivation and dissemination; the stricture, however, holds for the majority. One hears much of the impassiveness of the Hindus, but in England they show themselves much more excitable than Britishers and fall much more easily into extremes: infected with the virus of "modernity first, modernity second, modernity all the time," they become revolutionaries mainly because revolutionary principles are deemed modern, partly because a few intellectuals are revolutionaries. Many natives do their best to make it unpleasant for Englishmen resident in India, and in this they are

India, Charmian tended to side with the natives, Wilfrid definitely supported the British policy. "One would like to think with you, Charmian, but these people would be at a loss what to do with complete liberty if they were to get it. Yours is the view-point of idealism, but the hard facts bear out the line I have taken. I can't help thinking that the best form of government for India is a benevolent dictatorship, and I don't see any other nation carrying it into execution as efficiently, as kindly, as we do. The 'Reds' of both India and Great Britain complain bitterly and violently about 'domination,' whereas we act here with a forbearance that would put the average Christian to shame."

They then journeyed south to Ceylon, where they had almost a week in which to visit Kandy, several of the smaller towns, and Colombo itself. They passed two days in Colombo, where, living at the Galle Face Hotel, they spent the first morning in the Cinnamon Gardens, to which they took a rickshaw, thus rendering themselves fair game for all the pestering beggars of the district, children addressing them as *Farder* and *Mudder* and pointing with cleverly-simulated self-commiseration to their patently well-filled bellies or, more honestly, to their disgusting sores, importun-

often instigated by those whom Englishmen have tried to make comfortable in England. Before the Indian Mutiny, we tended to consider this country as existing for our especial benefit, nowadays the Indians seem to think that we exist for theirs. Perhaps it is some recondite form of equity and fair play to turn against one's educators and protectors; perhaps it is "good form" to repay hospitality with treachery. The Indians seem to forget what we do for them in all times of distress. Self-government is the wide-spread cry. If India were given absolute self-government, the various castes, races and tribes would soon be engaged in an internecine warfare, the issue of which would be that they supplicate the English to return; or perchance the Bolshevists would be called in with results somewhat different from those for which they bargained.

ate and fawningly-loquacious men, women holding out their naked babies ; where they drove by taxi-cab that afternoon to the Mount Lavinia Hotel, passing on the way village and forest, clumsy carriages and light drays of an antique form, natives doing their needs by the roadside, and on arriving at the hotel, they ordered tea on the delightful terrace ; where the following morning saw them shopping and visiting the native market, the afternoon found them motoring through another district by a less-known road, past wilder forest and by paddy-fields to tea again at Mount Lavinia. The glorious trip to Kandy through jungle and cultivated ground was made by motor, for that is the best way. There they visited temple and ruins ; if Colombo is modern, Kandy is mediæval Ceylon. From Kandy they proceeded to the west coast, whence they returned to Colombo the evening before the boat was to sail.

Three days out from that city, ship's sports were held. The afternoon passed pleasantly. The evening, though comparatively cool, was yet oppressive. Charmian sat in a secluded part of the deck, and with her was her lover : not her confirmed, but in spirit and desire as well as by one incident, her genuine lover. That last night at Colombo, they had strolled past the swimming bath of the hotel, down to the sea and along to the left. Such a mild, glamorous night as that applies a spark to passion already primed for action if opportunity but offer. Charmian appeared slightly languorous, Wilfrid had suffered from the continual restraint to which he subjected his longing : to tell the truth, she had not made things too easy for him, for sometimes when he put his arms about her, she snuggled close and seemed to be his if only he would urge. After walking a short distance they sat down in a depression, behind a sand dune. The inclined slope invited them to lean against it; doing so, they found themselves in an almost recumbent position. Charmian coloured slightly, but, with his arm supporting her, the night so glorious, the air warm and seductive, she did not attempt to rise. Silence, and the silent stars. Mouth sought mouth, they moved instinctly closer. He slipped one arm about her shoulders and with the other pulled her against him. Her eyes grew soft and melting, her cheeks a dull red, as her body was crushed to his; she trembled as he fondled her; the restless embrace suddenly became tense and significant, the tide of desire swept them swiftly along; they strained passionately each to each, with long warm kisses the while; a hand caressed her, now with a curiously restrained yet unmistakable and compelling ardour, now with a light playful touch or a delicate stroking, now again with a troublous closing of the fingers on her flesh. She responsively crumpled against him with a shiver and a long-drawn sigh as he throbbed in turbulent ecstasy. "Oh, Charmian, I love you," he whispered. "I believe you do, my dear. And I'd be a shameless hussy if I didn't love you!"

After lying some time longer in his arms, she remarked quietly: "I feel cold. Let us be going." Before they returned, however, she tidied her hair, smoothed out her frock, and ran her cambric handkerchief over her face. In these little matters, women are more fastidious than men.

Perhaps the memory of that evening was very much

with them as they sat in deck-chairs, sheltered from the wind and beyond prying eyes. Wilfrid considered that an audience was superfluous: his passion for Charmian was profound, all-engrossing: therefore he set the chairs so that, unflankable, they faced a corner projection-caused, with the backs towards anyone who might chance to promenade that way; the ship had few passengers, and those few were mostly present at an impromptu concert. The chairs were side by side. They had not found the opportunity to meet that day as they would have wished. "At last," murmured Wilfrid, as he took her in his arms. The kiss recompensed him for the long waiting, but it disturbed him too, for it was at once yielding and aggressive, soft and burning; her mouth melted against his. They stirred to a closer embrace, his free hand moved to her knee, to the firm flesh just above it, and pressed it with the unreflecting, natural persuasiveness of profound passion. He drew her, unprotesting, on to his own chair, capacious it is true, but not so wide that any other than an intimate propinquity was possible. Her eyes were veiled as with a filmy mist, his were hot and bright. She reclined voluptuously against him, he kissed her with increasing warmth and instancy, nor did she lag behind. In passionate encounters, when the man and woman are equally in love, there would seem to be a latent dislike for unreciprocated words, movements and caresses. With an inarticulate endearment, he encircled her yet more narrowly, as his kiss became more intimate, unconsciously audacious. She shrank a little; he thought that he had offended her. "Sorry, dear; I just couldn't help it!" She made no reply:

the gesture had perturbed her more than he could guess. A moment or two later, she drew his face down to hers and repaid him with a similar kiss, whereby all his doubts were stilled, all his lover's anxiety removed.

He sat thinking for several minutes. His cabin, by one of those coincidences which do sometimes happen outside the pages of a book, was next to hers, which gave directly on the sea; his had a recess for the port-hole. The cabin opposite to hers was occupied by a deaf old lady, while nobody had taken that opposite his. These four were all that opened on a short corridor running off a main passage. The situation was such that, to be quite frank, he could desire and think of only one thing. He leant over her, and, in low, broken voice, he murmured: "Charmian, shall I come to your cabin to-night at twelve?" She was silent for a moment, which to him lengthened to an hour. She rose slowly, and began to walk away. "Don't follow me now, dear one. *Au revoir*: till eleven o'clock, not midnight." "Darling," he whispered eagerly. She was gone.

He looked at his watch. Only ten! He walked up and down restlessly, his blood pulsing rapidly through a body that seemed to tread on air, his heart wildly exceeding its normal beat: at his lips was a song, a melody unheard by all save him: in his eyes shone a deep, all-enveloping joy. He moved to the side and watched the waters swirling by, gleaming in patches where phosphorescence played its part in the beauty of a tropical sea; the patches glowed faint and mysterious in the moonlight. Charmian joyed in the ocean thus lit up by the moon, he liked it best on a moonless, star-bright evening, when the water had its delicately-sombre hues and the phosphorus stood out sharply from, even while it fused with, the blues and greens around. Just now, however, he preferred the night to be thus wondrously moon-lit, for it accorded better with his happiness. Beyond the wash of the ship, the sea was like a mill-pond. The level stretches of water (rather than the broad expanse of ocean, for strips of shadow divided it here and there) glittered like burnished silver and then became soft of hue, fading at last into the dim and misty horizon. The sky was a vast inverted bowl of a strangely-smooth, faintly-silvered, most lovely, mellow radiance. The world had lost its ugliness, the vessel its hard lines, and Cunningham felt as if he stood in another sphere, a demesne of the moon, a region of faery. But passion coffered by memory and subtilised by absence better appreciates and enjoys such a scene than passion expectant can possibly do, for the latter, in its full-blooded joy, tends to miss the nuances and the overtones.

He descended to his cabin. Half an hour yet. How could he fill the time ? Much too excited to read. He put on his pyjamas and dressing-gown, thrust his feet into a pair of soft slippers, and went to the bathroom, where he treated himself to eighteen inches of water, a vigorous wallowing, and a brisk rub-down. He returned to his cabin, brushed his hair, looked at his watch again. Five minutes to go. Why hadn't he taken longer at his bath ? He picked up a book ; a citation of the most intimate passage in *The Song of Songs* caught his eye and held it. The ship's bells announced that it was eleven o'clock. The distance to Charmian's cabin was only ten feet: to him it seemed a mile as he went to his own door, but barely the ten feet when, sure that the coast was clear, he strode rapidly and silently to where, clad in a filmy kimono, she lay in welcome. He thought of Daudet's *Sapho* and wondered if between his desire and its consummation there intervened only that wrapper. As he sat on the edge of the bed, put one arm round her, and kissed her, he slipped his hand beneath the uppermost fold, perceived the warm flesh to be uncovered by jacket or gown, and, reverently, he cupped a lovely breast: the prisoner throbbed at the touch of tingling palm and gently-caressing fingers. She stroked his hair and drew his head down to the warmth of her throat, where he pressed his lips to that bewitching and sensitive spot a little below the ear. (Damn! Why should his mind recall the incident in Douglas Sladen's novel, *The Admiral*?) He raised his head, kissed her tenderly on both eyes, and then, uttering her name with a choking voice, set his lips between her breasts, which he held against his burning cheeks: her two hands clasped the nape of his neck, held him close and long. "Put out the light," she whispered with a passion that enchanted him; like most other modest, decent men in a similar case, he felt unworthy of his guerdon. He did as she asked. But before he rejoined her, he turned away in the penumbra to remove the garments that oppressed him; she too had stirred before he lay down beside her. Mouth clung to mouth, and form to form. A radiant smile lit up each face as they realised that now at last they could express unhindered their yearning, their adoration. Her breasts intoxicated him, and long did he joy in their perfect contour, their satin-firmness, as his senses took their fill ; lingeringly at times, fiercely at others, he drained their sweetness. She stirred to his caress and to the playing of his hand about her waist. Lips clung again ; no brotherly kiss was that. "Charmian," he whispered, "do you remember that poem by Eric Mackay ? *Three Kisses.* He was wrong, dear : the one he denounced is wonderful."

"It is, my darling. Soon after I met you, I dreamt of such a kiss and to-night you have made it real."

They were silent and still for a moment. His mouth sought her lips, her neck, her shoulders, while he resumed his caressing of that divinely-moulded body. With a low moan she fondled him in similar fashion. He thrilled, as, unconsciously, he caressed her yet more intimately. . . . . To describe the caresses that followed were to desecrate the shrine of man's desire. Charmian struggled a moment, apparently reluctant, longing unutterably, to accept the universal prelude of love's coming to perfection. Entranced, quivering, emulous, she murmured with rapture, until they sank into each other's arms, foredone and motionless for a time. But passion rests not content at this stage in its gamut of ecstasy, and, ere long, they clasped again. He grew rigid against her, she moulded herself to him, they became as one and joyed in their nearness.

. . . .

. . . .

But even the exultation of lovers must cease at the resumption of the daily round, and after a long, sweet, inactive embrace, they parted.

Three nights later, Charmian re-welcomed her lover to her arms. They had been very tender to each other in the interval and contrived to obtain some clandestine moments for a close enfolding, a prolonged kiss, an incipient caress. They were anhunger for more intimate contacts. She was never to forget that night, for, soon after he joined her, he kissed her troublously with suasive lips : she fought a brief space against such urgency, a love so intoxicated and so avid of fulfilment, such ravished longing and so complete a merging of his self in the passion that she evoked : this, a resistance of which convention is ignorant, was destined to be shattered as much by the force and convincingness, the tenderness and ardour of the tribute, as by her own response, soon elicited, increasingly intimate, utterly overwhelming : she yielded to the ultimate caress with the abandon of an intense and candid passion that is based on entire understanding and selfless love.

The days that ensued were as a dream, a trance. Love swayed their lives and informed their waking thoughts and sleeping visions. As they approached Melbourne, however, the sea rose one evening at the hest of a gale. Charmian went below. But Wilfrid, who enjoyed a storm, made himself comfortable in the smoking-room. Now and again he walked to the door to see how high the waves were running. After a brandy, which he took to banish the effect of the sudden chill in the air, he peered out ; the wind appeared to have dropped, the surge to have become a swell. He carefully crossed the slippery deck to the rail and gazed at the black, angry waters. Suddenly the wind rushed on the ship as it rounded a promontory, a huge wave swept the deck and dashed Wilfrid, caught wholly off his guard, against a capstan, where he lay stunned until the next billow carried him high over the iron-work into the night. An acquaintance in the smoking-room wondered if anything had happened to him ; he looked out and saw only the darkness. Uneasy, he searched the ship and reported his fears to the captain. Those suspicions were verified ; the body was never found. Meanwhile, Charmian slept soundly, wearied by love. But the crash of a mighty sea momentarily awoke her ; she shivered with an undefined dread ; and slept again.

VERNON DITCHLEY

VERNON DITCHLEY

VERNON DITCHLEY, except for three weeks in August, spent his time moving about ; a fortnight in London, then a fortnight in the provinces, wet weather or fine, good business or doldrums. Like many another, he had left a good job when he enlisted in 1914, and, when he returned to his firm as a lucky survivor the post was no longer vacant : " Awfully sorry, Ditchley! Perhaps in six months' time . . . ." That period having elapsed, the post was still being held down by a " conchy." He had, in 1917, become an officer, but he lacked money. After trying half a dozen temporary jobs he obtained the representation of a London publishing house, whose directors he had pleased with his attractive carriage and manners, his physical fitness, his easy and cultured speech, his knowledge of books, and his keenness. He was put on probation for three months; he made good ; now, in February, 1926, he had been five years with Messrs. Impress and Amusem, an old firm with a good general publishing list : travels and memoirs, a few solid books, occasional reprints of sure-winning classics, rare but excellent volumes of belles-lettres, and new novels (perhaps twenty-five each year) : a reputation for clean, wholesome, spirited stories, for something entertaining or worth-while in the other works. Not a spectacular or meteoric business, not a mincing-machine for trash, not one of those gilt-edged houses which can issue books in August with the same assurance as in October or March, not a specialised concern, but a typically English proprietary.

Although trusted and liked by his firm, which had recently hinted that, if he wished, he could have the London " beat " all the time, he was dissatisfied. He was, moreover, a little depressed, this bitterly cold February morning, for he had been visiting the booksellers of Induston, of whose inhabitants it is said that, after death, the better go to hell and the worse return to Induston. The booksellers were all decent fellows, but, by their own account, their trade, as usual, was so bad that only some miraculous intervention of the god of reading could have saved them from bankruptcy. One of them had exclaimed : " It's a pity you fellows—or your bosses—couldn't pass six months in a bookshop! You'd talk differently then."

" Admittedly ; but wouldn't a similar period in a publisher's office likewise benefit a bookseller ! "

Ditchley was too discreet to hint that while the average publisher would probably make a good bookseller, the average bookseller would make only half a publisher. He had once broached this subject with a friend, who pointed out that although he was justified in his main contention, yet there existed a few booksellers who, to a restricted extent, were also publishers. Ditchley assented readily : " Yes, and they generally issue very interesting books. But, after all, they are very few indeed." He was perhaps not so conversant with the difficulties of book-selling as he should have been. In many country shops, and in some elsewhere, the assistants might just as well have been selling butter as books, for all the interest they took in them.

In far too many shops, ignorance would seem to be considered tantamount to an ability to sell men's thoughts and dreams, their aspirations and imaginings, their personalities and souls, the fruit of years of study or of fervid and conscientious writing. "I confess," said Ditchley once to a delightful old bookseller, "that many of us travellers, 'bagmen,' as you call us, are just as bad: we seldom read the books we vaunt as *epoch-making* or *remarkable*, *the latest*, or *the best thing on the subject*; we speak of a 'Della Lethaby' or a 'Garbage' as if it were a 'Montague' or even a 'Hardy'; we 'unload' where and when we can: in fact, we are partly to blame for the scepticism of the booksellers. But, my friend, that scepticism often results from disappointment, that disappointment from inefficiency. If, anywhere outside of London, Oxford and Cambridge, Edinburgh and Glasgow, where there are bookshops that one would wish no different, an American bookstore were to commence business, it would wake up the whole trade to a startling degree. You would be forced to get a 'live' staff, well-informed, courteous and keen. Then you would increase your profits considerably. The success of the booksellers would, of course, mean the prosperity of publishers and the benefit of authors." The old man agreed; after a few minutes' silence, he asked: "Perhaps there are particular points that you would suggest as requiring redress?"

"I should think there were! I could name booksellers who, when they have sold all their copies of a book—not, mind you, an ephemeral novel or a piece of topical journalism, but a book that is as likely to sell three years hence as now—refuse to re-order simply because they are 'glad to see the back of it.' Far too many booksellers (they are, in fact, the huge majority) consider that, so far from it being in the least 'up to' them to push a book to try to sell it, it is the publisher's duty to advertise a book so heavily that people will come in and ask for it: in other words, they would seem to believe that their shops are merely entrepôts, that they are justifying their existence if they 'pass on' a book from publisher to public. The exceptions merit all praise: to travel a book to a genuine book-*seller* is a pleasure; to the other kind, a discouraging and tedious routine. Then look at the prevalent notion that poetry never sells: any thinking man knows that it sells much less readily than a 'key,' sensational, or lewd novel, but how many booksellers make an honest effort to persuade the public to buy it? And talking of novels, it is like squeezing through the proverbial eye of a needle to succeed in convincing certain booksellers that a first novel might easily be mature work or that it may have great merit: 'a big name,' they will tell you, sells thousands of copies of an inferior novel, an unknown author is a drug on the market—in the former case, the vendor hands out the book in dozens, while in the latter he has to go to the fatigue of recommending it. Moreover, the book of a famous author, whether it be good or bad, has a tremendous advantage over that of a newcomer, however good, for not only does the public, having eagerly anticipated, crowd after it and the press 'boost' it, but the bookseller gives it a window, whereas to the other he will hardly give a chance—unless the publisher is launching an advertising campaign."

"Perhaps," replied the veteran bookseller, "one could lay a few complaints about the publishers. Some of them seem to think that the publication of a book is synonymous with, or inevitably entails, its success. Some believe that a really good book will sell itself, but, unfortunately, this is untrue: normally, a good book unadvertised, or unnoticed (or little noticed) in the press, is simply swamped in the stream of mediocre publications."

"But," interposed Ditchley, "surely it is part of a bookseller's business to do his best for the good books!"

"You are paying the trade a compliment, which some of us try to deserve. For while many, I fear, don't care in the least whether a book is a masterpiece or sheer rubbish so long as it sells, there are others who honestly endeavour to give the good book a chance, who recommend it while they remain silent about the inferior volume. But one of the most serious problems of modern bookselling is the multiplicity of books: no one man can read more than a very small proportion of what he hopes to sell. In a big shop, of course, there are separate departments; there, it is easier for the assistants to have a tolerable knowledge of the volumes around them. And that brings me to another charge I have to make against publishers: they think that we should stock every book they issue."

"Yes, some publishers do expect too much. But you must agree that they are rightly annoyed at an incident like this:—Some time ago, I was travelling in the provinces. I went to the largest book-shop in a big town up North and showed the second novel of a very able writer. He is not famous, his first book had only a slight success, but the second was really good. No, the buyer wouldn't order a copy. A little later in the year I stayed a couple of days in that town, where I am known. Several acquaintances took me to task : 'You know that book you advised us to read ? We went to X.'s and they didn't have it in stock! So we passed to the next bookshop and bought it there.' Do you think that X. then ordered copies of the book ? Never in your life! He would have ordered it if the customers had asked him to obtain it for them, in which case he would pocket the discount for having been so energetic as to get the book from the publisher ; but he wouldn't take a sporting chance, even though several excellent reviews had appeared."

"He was probably afraid that the novel's slight, brief popularity would pass and leave him high and dry with copies on his shelves : and, as you know, the life of the average novel is reckoned at three months."

"Yes," conceded Ditchley, "that is true if the author writes no more books or never becomes well-known ; but if he achieves fame or even a small measure of popularity, the 'back numbers' usually benefit by a reflected glory. It must occasionally happen that a bookseller has on his shelves copies of the first edition of a publication that goes very slowly for six months or a year ; he forgets about the book—when he's not cursing it ; and then wakes up one spring morning to find that the original 'seven and sixpenny' now commands fifteen shillings or a guinea."

"That happy instance is one amongst scores of unfortunate experiences. It wouldn't do for us to buy copies of every first edition on the chance that they might become valuable! Of all the novels issued, I suppose only one in twenty requires a second printing, while five would probably be a generous estimate for the annual number of British novels whose first edition ' appreciates ' at all."

" True, but that is where it pays a bookseller to read at least a few of the books he buys—whether novels or belles-lettres."

" Most good booksellers make an attempt to do this."

" I'm glad to hear it ; I knew, of course, that you and one or two others did. Then what about limited editions ? "

" There are two kinds : the expensive limited edition of a great and famous living author—or perhaps he is only famous—alongside huge printings in a cheaper form ; and the publications of a firm specialising in restricted editions, mostly reprints. A risky business for the bookseller, both because a large number of these books, mere curiosities of literature, wouldn't sell more than fifty copies if they were issued in the ordinary way, and because collectors are kittle cattle."

" Well, my firm occasionally publishes limited editions."

" Yes, but they are of books that would sell in any case! No publisher will continuously succeed who does not remember that, however pleasant and however desirable it is to have good printing and binding, the primary test of a book is the excellence or the interest of the contents."

Ditchley was silent for a moment. " I wonder," he resumed thoughtfully, " what would happen to that publisher who, willing to forgo the profits of unlimited editions, issued good, but thoroughly readable, books—the kind that might appear on any well-known and respectable firm's general list—in limited editions ? "

" Either he would go bankrupt or, when once they recovered from the shock and pierced his dark intent, the booksellers and public would warmly approve; but I can't imagine any sane man voluntarily depriving himself of reasonable profits and taking the risk. He would be regarded as a revolutionary innovator : therefore worthy of distrust : therefore suspect. He would have to overcome several prejudices as deeply-rooted as they are stupid : for instance, that an old novel is dry ; that, indeed, any old book is dry ; or (with a self-contradiction characteristic of half-baked opinions) that a firm issuing numerous reprints has no right to publish new work ; moreover, that if this new work is in a limited edition, there must be something wrong with it. Business men would be sceptical and ' play safe ' ; and although the others would applaud, very few of them would help."

This cold and sensible reasoning sent a chill to Ditchley's heart. He had been thinking of starting a small publishing business with his practical knowledge and a legacy that he had lately received, but acknowledged that he did not possess the necessary courage to become a martyr. " Travelling " was now distasteful. He decided to give rein to a long-formed desire that represented a more radical trait of his character. With his £150 per annum, he could live, even if he met with no success for a time : he allowed himself three years in which to become known.

Early in March 1926 he resigned from Impress and

Amusem's. Having resisted the allurements of Hampstead, he took an unfurnished room in Bloomsbury and, with some spare funds, he set about furnishing it as a bed-sitting room ; a divan served as a bed, his books ranged one wall ; he had a gas-fire with a ring at the side. His breakfast he would get for himself ; lunch and dinner would draw him from his work to a cheap restaurant or café ; if he wanted a light supper, he had sufficient supplies in his own larder.

He had never done any writing. Educated at Westminster School, he proceeded thence to an advertising-agency, where his career was cut short by the war. But he had always been a steady reader ; his experience of life was adequate ; and he had a penetrating, wide-glancing mind of his own, a sense of humour, a gift for close observation of scene and character, a profound sympathy with his fellow-men, and an imagination at once romantic and realistic ; he loved beauty, but he did not on that account judge ugliness by its surface ; he desired happiness but was familiar with suffering ; he was neither sensual nor ascetic ; he strove to play the game. It was the composition, the writing itself which would form the greatest difficulty. At school, in English essays, he had usually ranked about fifth in his form : " Interesting, intelligent work, Ditchley," his master once said ; " but you seem to lack facility and you certainly lack style." But with the increase of knowledge and the development of his powers he felt that the facility would be greater ; for some years he had read with the thought at the back of his mind that, if ever he were to have the chance of putting into execution his pet idea, it would be well if he were previously equipped in the matter of vocabulary; practice, constant practice, to ease the joints of composition, would have to wait. His preparatory reading, which he continued when he set up to become an author, was to some extent systematic. He studied Strong's wonderful *Short History of English Literature* and such books on recent literature as Harold Williams's account of the writers of 1890-1914 and Manly and Rickert's *Contemporary British Literature* in order to learn which books it might help him most to read and con. Chiefly novels and short stories, with occasional excursions into history and belles-lettres. He revelled in the eighteenth-century novelists, whose directness appealed to him; he read or re-read Scott, Dickens, and Thackeray; he delved deep in Meredith, Trollope, and Hardy; he esteemed *Lorna Doone* a masterpiece of good Saxon English; he enjoyed Bennett and Galsworthy; he paid particular attention to the modern novelists. He considered that Hawthorne and Poe, Bret Harte and Bierce were worthy of close attention, especially for their short stories. He perused slowly and appreciatively the magnificent sweep of Gibbon, the clarity of Macaulay, and the eloquent energy of Froude, all of whom he examined for their narrative. Lamb the quaint, Hazlitt the vivid, and Leigh Hunt the gracefully sportive; Dr. John Brown and Matthew Arnold, Andrew Lang and Dobson, Chesterton and Belloc, Alice Meynell and Lucas, in their widely differing ways, formed his style and composition in essay and sketch. For the purposes of exposition, he learnt much from John Henry Newman. He began and ended by preferring a nervous Saxon style to any other, but, recognising the value of a more Latinised manner for certain kinds of writing (for instance, he had the strange notion that a formal dialogue might be used with advantage in the novel and even in a variation of the short-story form), he read with equal assiduity and delight the chief works of Sir Thomas Browne, Walter Savage Landor, De Quincey, and, in a lower rank, John Addington Symonds. In order to derive full benefit from a study of the best French prose-writers, he passed six "winter" months in Paris, perfecting his already tolerable knowledge of the language. To avoid dispersal of effect, he concentrated on eleven writers: Voltaire, Diderot, Rousseau, Vigny, Musset, Balzac, George Sand, Renan, Flaubert, Maupassant, and Anatole France, who supplied him not only with models of various departments of prose but with provocative exemplars of the novel, the middle-length and the short story: of these masters he was to continue his study for many years. Needless to say, his mind was immeasurably enriched by the combined subtlety and force of their writings, while his style improved beyond recognition in precision, his composition in orderliness, his argumentation in economy, his narrative in alertness. But, true to his nationality, he made his study of French and of French literature subserve his cultivation of English. He learnt what he could from a few writers of other countries, yet, as he knew no other foreign language than French, he could not, from the translations, pick up ideas on style; but the larger issues of structure, characterisation, plot, were analysed exhaustively. He even refreshed his Latin to read Cicero and Livy, Tacitus and Cæsar, while he resorted to translations of Greek to derive what benefit he could from Thucydides and Herodotus, Demosthenes, Plato, and the " novelists."

He was not, however, a confirmed theorist: he used no manuals on composition or style; no treatises on the art of the novelist or short-story writer: what he sought in the books that he read in order to become an author, not a paltry scribbler, was practical illumination, helpful example, suggestions and provocations: he had heard that exceedingly few theorists on style attained to eminence as stylists. Always, as he prosecuted his studies, he pushed on with his writing. At first he attempted sketches and light articles; then short stories; then, a year after his Rubicon, a novel. Some of the shorter compositions he destroyed immediately, some he submitted to an author-friend and then destroyed; six articles, sketches, or stories were all that survived from the first twelve months' work. These he sent to various editors: an unimportant provincial newspaper accepted one article, an important London daily a playful sketch of a tenderfoot's impressions of Paris, and a high-brow magazine (mistaking a caricature of Crackanthorpe for " advanced " gloom) a short story, for which, since the periodical was wound up three months later, he received no payment and not even the glory of publication. Not a reckoning on which to base roseate dreams of fame or wealth. But his modest competence, sparing him the harassing fears of starvation, allowed him to persevere undisturbed; his confidence was undiminished, his modesty unimpaired. One editor had praised his character-drawing, another his fresh and unaffected narrative. He was learning, also, where and when to place his manuscripts, what payments were customary, and what were the ins-and-outs of copyright. He had no intention of being "easy money" for either editors or publishers.

He permitted himself two hobbies. One was the relation of reviews to advertisements: he rejoiced to see that the best periodicals noticed books irrespective of the advertisements in their columns, but grieved to hear from a hard-bitten old journalist that certain newspapers and magazines always or usually gave the preference to advertised books; a publisher-acquaintance disclosed the mysteries of the allocation of the best positions and amused him by explaining the nature and uses of "keyed" advertisements. The other was the art or the haphazardry of reviewing. He perceived that while some periodicals were prompt, others were exceedingly slow to review, and while some gave books to suitable men, others handed them to an indifferent staff. He soon discovered that while certain critics discussed impartially, others were swayed by political, religious, philosophic or a kindred bias; some confined themselves to the book in question, others ranged heaven and earth; some recommended the public to read, others seemed bent on frightening it away; several made a point of saying that the book should have been quite different from what it was or should have contained matter related to, and clearly indicative of, their own particular hobby-horse; some tried to be clever, others cynical; some used quotations unfairly, and some even victimised an author or a publisher—or both—merely to increase the sales of their periodical by a shameless piece of "stunt" journalism.

He derived pleasure also from wandering around the bookshops, new and second-hand. When he did not go to London's wonderfully situated best bookshop, where he enjoyed the courteous and efficient service, he frequented either the small but intriguing places within a thousand yards' radius of the British Museum, or the equally small and distinctive shops in Chelsea and its environs, for he liked to talk with the cultured, whole-hearted book lovers who presided over the modest but enticing and usually well-presented stock of books. London's smaller bookshops are a study in themselves: they are conducted by men who are pleasant and extremely well-read, sometimes by women who are modern and charming: they merit a monograph from the pen of an Augustine Birrell or a Michael Sadleir. One would naturally begin with the postal districts known officially as W.C.1. and S.W.3; then one might profitably hunt for the nooks of W.8 and E.C.4; while several of the outer suburbs contain a delightful surprise. Possibly this monograph would lead to another on what one might call the cultured bookshops of central London: Old and New Bond Street and their vicinity, Charing Cross Road, King William Street, The Strand, Queen Street. The great circulating libraries, with the *Times* Book Club at their head, deserve a brochure to themselves. Those three monographs could be written by either a book lover, a publisher, or a well-educated and widely-read "traveller"; but the first of these could not handle the equally illuminating companion-booklets on the pair of combines whose names are proverbial, nor the pamphlet on the growth and influence of the export-booksellers. An enterprising publisher—he must have been one of those men who joyously sniff the battle from afar—invited Ditchley to undertake the whole series, to which he proposed to add an imposing volume entitled: *Some British Bookshops outside London*. But Ditchley refused, not because he shrank from the jealousy and recrimination that might arise for the publisher or even because he feared lest some of the offended persons (for the truth, however tactfully administered, would probably infuriate a certain small number) would boycott his own books when they should appear, but simply because he wished to devote himself mainly to creative writing.

His novel gave him less trouble than he anticipated; it was written in seven months (including three for research), corrected and finalised in two more. Three hundred pages of double-spaced typewritten quarto. Subject: a romance of Birmingham, with its main action beginning in the year 1800. Treatment: wholly imaginary in the incidents and characters; the background, sparingly historical. The story flowed clear, unencumbered, unimpeded, like a river that has its own way with us despite the beauty or the interest of the banks and shores; it proceeded straight to the sea, without forming backwaters or lagoons on its journey, in contradistinction to those tales in which the narrative either toils painfully through the silty flatlands of the "history" or looks like a lumber-stream, so many are the subsidiary incidents and rank excrescences. Ditchley had attempted to make the characters self-illustrative; by skilful, natural, intimate dialogue he showed every trait. Of psycho-analysis there was none, of modern cleverness there was no trace; Freud's influence was null. Love and passion were treated with the refreshing directness of Fielding: he eschewed glorification equally with belittlement; he wrote neither up to society's prudery nor down to man's prurience. He drew no moral, and he stated no political nor historical conclusions. The principal character was shown as boy and youth in Birmingham, as a soldier in Spain, as a wounded hero returned and as the victim of hard times; there was an original but not an eccentric heroine; several rivals for her hand went as near to being "the villain of the piece" as its author could manage without caricature or improbability.

To write a novel is one thing, to get it published is another. He first sent off his manuscript at the beginning of November, 1927. Soon he learnt that if fiction be written by a wholly unknown person, and if, further, it be neither "sex" nor "society" novel, neither "detective" nor "ghost" story, it might spend a discouragingly long time in the hands of "readers," unless the author have an influential friend in a publisher's office. Several firms returned the manuscript very promptly; they could not possibly have read it, but they knew that it was "unsuitable." One house wrote: "We like your story very well. In fact, if you will change the last chapter, if you will turn that unnecessarily tragic conclusion into a more happy ending, we are prepared to consider it very favourably. We do not suggest that the close should see the hero and heroine 'blissfully happy,' but the hero might be spared that horrible death. We suggest for your consideration—as you are new to this kind of work—the irrefutable fact that even nowadays the great majority of readers dislike a sad ending. The reviewers will pick on this point, and the result will be smaller sales, therefore smaller royalties." Ditchley withdrew his manuscript immediately. Another publisher declared that he could not handle "historical novels," while a solid and respected firm, considering that the historical background was insufficiently developed, said: "This is neither an historical novel nor yet a straightforward tale of adventure." Still another rejected it on the ground that the circulating libraries would fight shy, since the frankness of the love-scenes was sure to offend. "Not enough plot," said Spenlow: "not enough characterisation," said Jorkins. Early in March, 1928, the author thought that, at last, the luck was turning: a well-known firm gave the manuscript to a "reader," who pronounced himself uncertain; a second reader declared that, although it had considerable merit, it was unlikely to pay expenses, let alone yield a satisfactory profit; a third found it "very promising"; a junior partner read it and decided against it. Ditchley was in despair. Then, as a forlorn hope, he despatched the manuscript to a publisher who, issuing perhaps a dozen novels a year, insisted on a high standard. At the beginning of May, it was accepted.

He could hardly believe his eyes, as he held the brief letter in trembling hands. He went to see the partner responsible for novels. The two men discussed certain details of publication and settled the matter to their mutual satisfaction. The contract was drawn-up and duly signed: *Henry Clark* was to appear in the middle of September. Although fittingly excited by the prospect of seeing his novel in print, Vernon Ditchley was not one to rest on his prospective laurels—if indeed they should prove to be enduring bays and not a withered chaplet. He wrote three short stories in the interval; two were accepted for publication by leading magazines of a literary tendency, one solely on its merits, the other because the publisher had mentioned Ditchley's name to his personal friend the editor.

At last *Henry Clark* came before the bar of public opinion. Its author viewed with trepidation the reading of the notices, for the book had "subscribed" only fifty copies in London and the same number elsewhere. "One hundred copies taken by the booksellers before publication is not very gratifying, Mr. Ditchley," observed the partner concerned; "we had hoped for better results." On seeing the author's crestfallen look and understanding his murmured regrets, he hastened to add: "But that is nothing against you; it is our misfortune. There is, however, plenty of time yet. The book was ready only this morning! You may be interested to learn that, several years ago, we published a novel that has reached the 25,000 mark, which is very good for so fine, so literary a book. Well, it 'subscribed' a hundred and twenty copies. And, mind you, it was the author's second work—although I admit that the first had met with only a very modest *succès d'estime*. Two months passed: perhaps three hundred had been sold by the end of that period. Then two big journalists specially noticed it; others followed, all vying with one another in praising it. The intelligent portion of the general public—a portion that I estimate at about 20,000 for Great Britain—flocked to buy this outstanding novel. The Colonies were infected with the like commendable anxiety. But there you are! We trust that your book will have an equally pleasing history."

Vernon Ditchley did not entertain any wild hopes. On the day of publication, a Friday, there was only one review; *The Daily Telegram* gave the book twenty lines of balanced yet most inspiriting eulogy. "As an historical novel," it said, "*Henry Clark* ranks with *Blue Athens* and *Colonel Rack* as the finest we have seen this year. As a novel without the qualifying adjective, it is certainly among the best half-dozen published since last September." The next day, two of the weeklies noticed it, one criticism being brief and neutral (it was one of those reviews that any man of ordinary education could write without opening the book); the other causing Ditchley's heart to pulsate rapidly, for, a column and a half in length, it praised the novel highly and, more significantly, it acclaimed the author, not only as a coming man, but as a definite and impressive arrival. "The sobriety with which the hero's character is implied must not blind us to the unobtrusive art that has gone to the making of an unforgettable figure. The heroine could hardly be better drawn than the hero, but she is in some ways more remarkable. The lissom and convincing dialogue, the sudden flashes of beauty displayed in scene and emotion, the noble simplicity of the structure, and that propulsion of narrative which can be compared only with the easy, deliberate, yet surprisingly fleet progress of an Olympic 'three miler': all these qualities stamp *Henry Clark* both as a work of great talent judged by any standard and as easily the finest first-novel of the year." From the most alert and provocative of all British weeklies, this was far more than the author had expected in his most sanguine moments. A week later, the book received an ambiguous paragraph from C.C. in *The Watcher* and a hearty and appreciative welcome from the equally witty Mr. Pellet in the *Sunday Period*. *The Literary Extra* stemmed the tide of favour by giving the novel eight mediocre lines in small print, but the *Morning Messenger*, the *Mancunian Thinker*, *The Yorkshire Clarion*, and nearly all the monthly reviews were, sooner or later, to join in the chorus of praise. The publishers seized the press by the forelock and improved its shining days by a discreet advertising campaign. In six weeks Vernon Ditchley was a celebrity among thoughtful readers; "the popular press" sought his photograph, literary societies his membership, cultured hostesses his presence at dinner; European literary agencies competed for translation rights, while American publishers suggested options on his next two works; most significant fact of all, perhaps, several hardened reviewers wrote to tell him what an oasis in the desert his book had been to them.

But he accepts few invitations and makes friends slowly. Success has spurred him to write a great novel: the one on which he is at present engaged may realise that hope. If not then, it will not be many years before he produces a masterpiece.

THE END